Murder Above the Fold

ReGina Welling

Erin Lynn

Murder Above the Fold

Copyright © 2018 by ReGina Welling and Erin Lynn

ISBN- 978- 1986093033

ISBN- 1986093034

Cover design by: L. Vryhof

Interior design by: L. Vryhof

http://reginawelling.com

http://erinlynnwrites.com

First Edition

Printed in the U.S.A.

Contents

Chapter One

"I like them." Margaret Balefire stretched herself into as menacing a posture as she could manage, narrowed her eyes and glared at her sister, Clara. She waggled a finger, and a set of lace doilies magically appeared on the shelf.

Not intimidated in the least, Clara lifted her nose in an upward gesture and shook her head. "I don't. They have to go."

She swiped her hand through the air, clearing the shelves, then continued lining the oak bookcase with sparkling bottles and jars. Each sported the store's distinctive label—the store name, *Balms and Bygones,* was emblazoned in silver and green across a complicated Celtic symbol and stood out nicely against a creamy background.

"We agreed you can arrange the antiques any way you like them, but the personal care products are my domain," Clara said, arranging the jars just so. "The jewel tones of these glass bottles look better against bare wood, and my products are meant for a younger market, so keep the hideous doilies away from my shelves."

If Margaret—Mag to her friends—had her way, everything in the shop would be covered in Victorian lace and frills. Her decorating tastes ran completely counter to the

5

staunch exterior she presented to the world and hinted at gentler emotions lurking beneath the prickly shell. Instead of arguing, she wrinkled her nose, waggled her hips, and flashed a rude hand gesture behind Clara's back. Hair aged to a dandelion-fuzz-like texture floated in the breeze created by the motion.

"I saw that," Clara said. "Mature. Real mature." Resisting the temptation to return the gesture took every ounce of her self-control. Instead, she swiveled a jar of face cream so the label faced front, and the ruby-colored glass picked up a shine from a strategically placed spotlight. After a moment's thought, she added a bar of soap in the same scent to the display. Heart, soul, and a dollop of true magic went into every drop of her ever-growing product line.

"If you're done communing with the display, we should get moving before we miss our appointment at the newspaper office. You have the photos, right?" Despite the tart delivery and emphasis on the words *communing with the display*, no real heat colored Mag's statement. If Clara wanted to show her wares on naked shelves, it was her choice.

"I've got everything right here." Clara brandished her cell phone.

"Should have known. That thing is practically melded to your hand these days. What self-respecting witch takes selfies, I ask you?"

"It's a handy organizational tool. You should get one." Like that would ever happen. "And it takes fantastic photos." To illustrate, Clara snapped one of the look on Mag's face and flipped the phone around so Mag could see the sneer of disdain. "My new screensaver."

Opening a shop together hadn't been the main reason the sister witches moved to the hamlet of Harmony, but the joint venture was turning out to be more interesting than either of them expected. The soft opening, about a month before, had

6

drawn in curious customers from miles away. Once people were inside the store, Clara's open smile and friendly ways combined with Mag's stash of antiques put people in the buying mood.

It helped that there was enough living space for them, too—Clara lived above the shop, and Mag lived behind it.

"Stop being grouchy," Clara said, breezing past her, "and I'll get you an ice cream cone on the way back. Dairyland opened today."

Mag scowled. "I'm not a ten-year-old, you know," she said, then sniffed and added, "You think they have butter pecan?"

Clara locked the door behind them, smiling and shaking her head.

Postcard-pretty, the town of Harmony hugged the southern bank of Big Spurwink River and, Mag insisted, possessed a seedy underbelly. But then, she harbored a bone-deep suspicion of almost everyone and everything, so her opinion was best taken with a grain of salt. Or twenty.

Summer leaves would soon hide all except for the barest glimpse of the river, but that day, a stand of white birch trees framed Clara's view of the rock-strewn banks perfectly.

Balms and Bygones was situated on Mystic Street, which meandered along Big Spurwink's banks before ending abruptly in a parking lot at the edge of the town square. Positioned in a place of honor at the far end of a grassy quad, Harmony's municipal office was the oldest standing structure in town.

C-shaped, the town-hall courtyard backed the second oldest structure in Harmony. The clock tower speared skyward and, especially during the summer months, tempted tourists off the main road for a prime photo opportunity.

On either side of the square, a bank of buildings housed shops, eateries, and offices. Today, Mag and Clara approached a brick structure with picture pane windows on the town's westerly edge—the one separated by the river by only a small back parking area and a steep embankment.

"Sorry, we're a couple of minutes late," Clara said to the harried-looking brunette who stepped up behind the tall counter spanning the front of the narrow space. "We had an appointment to discuss putting an ad in the paper."

"No worries," the woman said. "I'm Marsha Hutchins. You probably spoke to Leanne on the phone." The way her voice lifted made the statement sound like a question. "She usually handles setting up new ad accounts."

"We did. Is Leanne here? It looks like you have your hands full." Clara nodded toward a long table strewn with photographs, a few of which were arranged in a grid.

"Leanne went out on an errand." Marsha tucked a stray strand of hair behind one ear, a slight frown marring her forehead. "She should have been back by now. Anyway, what can I do for you?"

"I'm Clara Balefire, and this is my mother, Margaret." The lie tripped easily off her tongue, having repeated it in practice about a hundred times. Clara expected she'd slip up eventually, but given the assumed difference in age based on Mag's outward appearance, no sane person would buy the story of the two being sisters.

The blood-born power of magic slows the aging process and adds centuries to the lifespan of a natural witch unless she's the victim of a curse or magical disaster. Mag knew all about the kind of accident that could add years to a witch's face, but she didn't like to talk about her past much.

"We've recently opened a shop over on Mystic Street. You might have heard about us."

Gossip travels fast in small towns and any newspaper woman worth her salt would already know that a new business opened up. Marsha didn't disappoint.

"Oh, yes. Balms and Bygones. Antiques and personal care products. Whatever made you decide on that combination?"

"Playing to our strengths and interests." While Clara chatted pleasantly, Mag treated Marsha to the same level of scrutiny she did when meeting anyone new.

Shrewd senses ignored the slightly ruffled exterior to test the mettle of the woman underneath the surface. A thirst for truth balanced by a highly-developed sense of justice let Marsha pass the test.

This was a woman Mag could respect. Her dress got the elder witch's stamp of approval, too, since there was a tiny hint of lace peeking out around the neckline of the muted paisley print. Had they been shopping together, Clara would have been drawn to the garment based on style. She appreciated the way the cut of it hugged Marsha's curves while remaining work-appropriate.

"Leanne recommended using a half-page spread as an introductory piece, and then she wanted to talk about an ongoing placement where we could feature new items each week. In color." Clara whipped out her cell phone and started leafing through images.

"This is perfect timing since I'm working on the layout for a commemorative..." Before Marsha could finish, the sound of a slamming door and male voices issued from the rear of the building and interrupted her.

"Go left. No, your other left," said a gruff voice Clara recognized as Perry Weatherall's. Perry, though no witch himself, had ties to the organization that camouflaged the local coven.

"Dude, it's heavy. Where does she want it? Marsha, come here!"

Marsha huffed out a breath. "Excuse me, ladies, won't you? I'm sorry about this, I feel like a duck paddling backward today." Leaving that odd mental image, and tossing a second sorry over her shoulder, Marsha hurried toward the commotion in the back room. "In that corner. Watch out for..." Banging noises and grunts preceded a conversation about whether an industrial-sized printer would fit through the door.

Several minutes later, which Mag and Clara spent eavesdropping shamelessly, the back door slammed shut behind Perry, and Marsha popped back into view just ahead of a younger man who was wiping sweat on the sleeve of his Oxford shirt. Everything about him could best be described as average—height, weight, even the color of his hair landed in a nondescript shade between blond and brown. If not for the fact he was wearing neon-yellow cross trainers below the khaki pants, Mag might have thought him completely devoid of personality.

When he noticed the newcomers, he stepped up to the counter, loosed a gleaming smile, and whipped a card out of his pocket.

"I don't believe we've met. The name's Bryer Mack, and you'd be the ladies who bought Hagatha Crow's place. Good bones, that one. They don't build them like that anymore, you know. Foundation needed work, but I'm sure your agent told you all about it."

He might as well have made air-quotes around the word agent, and when his business card landed on the counter, Clara understood why. Mack owned a real estate office, a rival to the witch-owned agency they'd used.

His smile, artificially whitened though it was, seemed genuine. "Anyway, welcome to Harmony." His gaze roved over Clara's curves with interest.

She needed no magic to draw a man's attention; the curvy body, emerald eyes over rose-petal lips, and a lush cascade of chestnut hair were enough. Of the two sisters, Clara had been the one to take after the Balefire side of the family and was the spitting image of their mother.

Rather than feeling left out, Mag had always reveled in her mile-wide nonconformist streak and was proud to have taken her looks from their father: long and lean, without an ounce of spare flesh over a runner's frame, ginger hair, and pale skin that freckled in the sun.

Along with his looks, Mag had inherited her father's desire to see the world and his conviction that justice ranked higher than mercy. By right of birth, Mag should have become the keeper of the sacred Balefire flame instead of Clara, but it would have killed something inside her to be confined to home and hearth. Adventure called, and an eager Mag had answered.

Clara only knew bits and pieces of the rest of her sister's story. Somewhere out on the road, Mag encountered and defeated her first Raythe. Rare beasts born of untethered magic, they fed off the souls of witches and were devilishly hard to kill. Mag, it turned out, had an uncommon flair for defensive magic and spent her youth honing that skill at significant cost.

"Now, what was I doing?" Marsha shook her head to clear away the cobwebs. "Sorry. What I started to explain before the guys showed up is that I'm putting together the layout for a special edition of the paper. You're aware we're commemorating our town bicentennial this week, I assume." She waited for Clara's nod before continuing. "Your timing couldn't be better. Since I'm already late getting this to the printer, there's time to add your business as a sponsor if you're interested."

"I'd have thought you'd be using a computer for that type of thing." Clara indicated the table covered with images. "Digital seems to have taken over the world." Mag's snort went ignored.

"Call me old-fashioned, but I like to do the front page layouts of all our special editions by hand." This from a woman who looked barely old enough to remember the days when they printed papers on presses. "The way my grandfather taught me."

"To hear her tell it, ink runs in her family's veins instead of blood." Bryer skirted the table without looking at its contents and made his way to the far corner where a mini-fridge and coffeemaker sat on a 1950s-era sideboard with an aqua- and- black laminated top and frosted glass doors. Mag eyed the piece with disdain. Too retro for her tastes, even if Clara insisted there was money to be made from vintage furniture.

As though he'd performed the task a hundred times before, Bryer poured himself a cup of coffee, toasted Marsha with it, and delivered his parting shot, "There are half a dozen celebrations in this town every year, and they all get the special-edition treatment. Seems like you'd have a template ready;, I mean, how different can it be? Besides, no one is even going to bother looking at the same old pictures of the same old clock tower. Might be time to think up a new angle."

Marsha ignored the mild criticism, but not the insistent series of bing-bong sounds coming from the sleek laptop sitting in the corner of her layout table.

She shot a half-smile at the sisters. "If you'll excuse me for one moment." She muttered something impatient and mildly unflattering about Leanne's lack of punctuality as she hit a key to bring up her email.

"Tell her I'll be back with the proper cables in a few minutes, won't you?" Bryer flashed a smile toward Clara and Mag, then turned to leave the way he'd come in—through the back of the office. He cast an idle glance at the contents of the table as he passed by, paused to look back at Marsha, then strode out of the room.

"Can't anyone hit a deadline this week?" Marsha's fingers danced across the keyboard in rapid-fire movements for a minute, and then she flipped the screen down and returned her gaze to the sisters. "I really am sorry for being so distracted."

Marsha pulled a form out of her desk and laid it on the counter with a pen. "Here's what I can do. We'll bump you up to a sponsor level, give you a quarter-page ad. I know that's smaller than what Leanne quoted, but we'll move you up to page three, so it's big and bold, and right there when people open up the paper. We're expecting an exceptional turnout—at least triple our normal readership, so you'll receive plenty of exposure."

Ever the pragmatist, Mag cut right to the chase, "How much?"

Marsha named a price and went into a spiel about the forms of accepted payment.

Reasonable, Clara thought. She reached into her Hermione's purse of a pocket, fished around among potion bottles, a spare scarf for windy days, and pulled out a wad of crumpled-up cash. The sight of Clara smoothing the bills against the edge of the counter to get the wrinkles out brought a hint of a twitch to the corner of Marsha's mouth.

"Thank you for your business," she said, taking the money. "And if you're willing, I'd love to send one of my feature writers around for an interview that would run the next week as a follow-up piece. A mother and daughter moving to a new town and opening a business together makes for a great human-interest piece. I don't suppose either of you has a checkered past to spice things up?"

Taking a page out of Hagatha's book, Clara told the truth. "My mother," she cocked a thumb at Mag, "used to kill rogue hell beasts and I spent the last twenty-five years in prison for a crime I didn't commit." The utter dryness of her tone pulled a trill of laughter out of Marsha and even tweaked a grudging smile from Mag.

"Now, Clara," Mag scolded, "you know that's not completely accurate. Hell beasts are an entirely different species."

"What wonderful senses of humor. You'll want to hang onto them when tourist season gets into full swing." Turning back toward her layout, Marsha missed Mag's suppressed snort and Clara's waggling eyebrows.

"Anyway," Marsha continued, motioning for them to follow her. "I'm really excited about the special edition this year because we're celebrating two important anniversaries. Why don't you come take a look?" She flipped one hinged end of the counter up to let Mag and Clara pass through to the area behind the scenes.

Despite appearing a jumbled mess, there was a sense of order to the table holding Marsha's proposed layout. Two photos of the clock tower lay side by side in the spot Clara assumed would make up the main body of the front page and looked like one of those puzzles where players are invited to find the differences. Not that it would be difficult in that case.

Marsha tapped first one picture, then the other. "These were taken ten years ago. Before and after the restoration was completed."

In the first photo, the clock was missing both hands and several of the numbers. Peeling paint and sections of battered trim marred the wooden structure, and the peaked roof badly needed new shingles.

In contrast, the second image featured gaily colored banners festooned across pristine white paint below the fully restored clock Clara had admired earlier in the day. More banners decorated the town square, which was filled with people in the midst of a celebration.

Underlining the before-and-after shots, another series of images tracked the progress of the renovation.

"But, anyway," Marsha said, "part of the reason I'm so excited is that these photos were taken with an old pocket-sized camera that was past its prime long before the digital age, and the negatives were so small, every effort to blow up the images made them incredibly grainy. I found a company that specializes in digitally remastering old film and had a new set made. As you can see, they did a spectacular job." The pair of prints looked like day and night.

"Nice work on the clock. Must have taken weeks." Appreciative of older things, Mag found the restoration process heartening. She might have asked a question or two, but Marsha never gave her a chance. She pointed to the man with the tools, deepened her voice to a reverent tone, and said, Aldo Von Gunten, a name that meant absolutely nothing to the Balefire sisters.

"You've never heard of him?" She asked when neither oohs nor ahs were forthcoming.

"Can't say it rings a bell," Clara replied.

"He's a local man who's quite famous all over the world for his work with historical timepieces. I was sure he'd move away after what happened to his daughter. Absolutely tragic, the way she…" she pressed her lips tightly closed and allowed her words to trail off when Bryer Mack opened the front door, then stepped aside to hold it for a slip of a woman who came in like an apologetic whirlwind.

"I'm sorry," she said before she was even all the way inside. "So sorry. I'm a complete idiot, and you should fire me on the spot. I set up an appointment with those two women who——" Bright blue eyes magnified by an enormous pair of glasses turned toward Mag and Clara. "Are already here," she finished, sighing.

The new arrival scurried through the office, depositing a large purse and two reams of paper on the single island of clutter in the whole space—a desk across from the layout table.

Marsha blew out a breath. "Please tell me you at least got a check from Mrs. Mathers for your efforts. Wasn't that meeting set for 11:30? It's nearly two in the afternoon now."

If she had any qualms about discussing Leanne's lackadaisical attitude toward work in front of complete strangers, it was buried deep beneath a mound of irritation.

"Yes, of course, I got the check, and then I stopped by the office supply place." Leanne's cheeks pinked, and her voice faltered when she added, "and misplaced my glasses. It took forever to find them."

Mag raised an eyebrow. Anyone sporting lenses that thick ought to figure they'd need to be wearing glasses if they planned on finding anything. A circular problem if ever there was one.

"You really should consider wearing your contacts more often." Marsha looked like she wanted to say more, but didn't get the chance when the desk phone shrieked to life. Waving Leanne off when she reached for it, she said, "I'll get it. Take a look at the layout, I think it's ready to go."

"And that's my cue to fire up the printer," Bryer and Leanne moved in the same direction at the same time and nearly collided. When he placed a steadying hand on her shoulder, one of the restored photos caught his eye, and he picked it up so quickly it created a breeze that blew two others out of place.

On a sigh, Marsha picked up the phone. "Harmony Holler."

A loud, angry chatter streamed from the handset. Someone wasn't happy about something; that was for sure. Shrill tones rendered the words unintelligible, but the sentiment was crystal-clear.

The final words were clear, though. "You're gonna pay for this, you just wait and see!" Before Marsha had a chance to say another word, the line disconnected and she gently placed the handset back in its cradle.

The smile she turned toward the Balefire sisters gave no hint of her response to the threats and accusations she'd just endured. Gently, she ushered them back through the folding counter and toward the door.

"You ladies are all set. It was very nice to meet you, and I'll be in touch about that human interest piece." Her tone was filled with sincerity even though it was obvious she wanted to get on with whatever was next on her agenda.

As they exited, she heard Marsha say to Leanne, "Better call Dylan and tell him you're going to be working late."

"Speaking of—we should probably head back to the shop." Out of the corner of her eye, Clara watched Mag bristle. "After we stop for ice cream." She threaded an arm through her sister's and turned toward Dairyland and the promise of buttery-sweet, pecan-filled goodness.

On the way home, the clock tower caught Clara's eye. Armed with new knowledge, she appraised the structure. Ten years on, the paint could use a touch-up here and there, but the permanence of the symbol meant something to this town. She could see that, and felt good about making a life here among good people who would put so much care into making Harmony a better place to live.

Concentrating on that thought, Clara stepped off the curb and if Mag hadn't yanked her back at the last second, would have become another statistic. The breeze stirred by a passing motorcycle tossed her hair in her eyes, but not before she got a good look at the license plate. BRYGUY.

"Watch where you're going you jerk." Waving a gnarled fist in the air, Mag yelled at the retreating figure she recognized partly because it made sense given the vanity plate, but mostly when the neon flash of his footwear gave him away.

"That was close. Next time I see that Bryer Mack, he's getting a piece of my mind for speeding in town. Kid's bike, though. '77 Kawasaki KZ1000. Kind of machine a teenager might spend his summer income to buy. Still, any bike is better than none. I miss the feel of the wind in my hair." Mag's voice turned wistful even as she shocked her sister with the revelation and sparked a mental image Clara never expected to see.

Chapter Two

"You're late." Wearing a Santa Claus apron over a red, fur-trimmed dress and green-and-white-striped tights, Gertrude Granger bustled up as though she'd been hiding and watching for her impending guests to make their entrance. "Come with me." Smelling of cinnamon and vanilla, the wannabe elf dragged the Balefire sisters into the kitchen, where she whipped a batch of snowflake-shaped cookies out of the oven.

"*We're* late? Doesn't she know Christmas was months ago?" Mag hissed in Clara's ear.

"Shh. You'll hurt her feelings."

Whether she heard the whispered conversation or not, Gertrude never let on. Instead, she plied the sisters with peppermint cocoa, then hustled off to retrieve the table-top-sized antique sleigh she'd asked Mag to assess for value and sell on consignment at Balms and Bygones.

The thing was so ancient, Mag wouldn't have been surprised if it carried the maker's mark of old St. Nick himself. Since he'd given over to mass-produced goods, it was getting harder and harder to find an original Kringle.

"Figured you'd want to know Hagatha showed up here half an hour ago. I think she's up to something." Gertrude sat the piece down so the sisters could examine it closer.

I think she's up to something—a phrase the Balefire sisters had come to dread and the one most often uttered when Hagatha Crow's name came up in conversation.

"What is it this time?" No answer could shock Clara since Hagatha was capable of just about anything. "Levitating fire trucks? Enchanted candy? Flying, tutu-wearing pigs? Not that I don't enjoy crafting a good pig poop-banishing spell, but once was enough to last me a lifetime." And those were just the highlights.

"Funny how we were the only witches in a three-town radius with nothing better to do that day. Quite the coincidence," Mag pointed out. She suspected the witches of the coven were a little too happy to turn the Hagatha problem over to its two newest members and leave them on their own to deal with the fallout. Not what she'd signed on for when certain members had come begging the Balefire sisters to join their coven. Mag had been under the impression the group was looking for new leadership, not glorified babysitters for an old witch with too much power and no filter.

Gertrude feigned innocence. "Well, she's got a bee in her bonnet, and she's acting squirrely. More than usual." And that was saying something.

"Shocking. The woman wears a beehive for a hat on all the days that end with a Y and doesn't bother to hide her nuts for the winter. What is it this time? Is she planning on hexing the channel five meteorologists for predicting rain again?" Mag asked.

"No," Gertrude tapped her fingertips on the table as if talking about Hagatha made her nervous, "I don't think she'd try again after what happened the last time. She wanted me to go on the Internet and scour all the auction sites for as much ulexite as I could find. Ulexite, of all things!"

"Television stone," Mag told Clara. She had a catalog of useful information in her head. "When sliced crosswise and polished, it has fiber optic properties. In magic, it's used for displaying images. Not a stone often called for in general casting, but useful for projecting during divination. Wonder what she plans to do with large quantities of it."

"No idea." Gertrude lowered her voice, a sure sign she was about to impart some juicy gossip. "But that's not the only thing I've heard. Penelope told me Perry Weatherall came to the center this morning, and he and Hagatha had a huge fight over who gets to use the folding tables. Perry says the Badgers need them for the auction and, of course, Hagatha insisted we had dibs on them for the tag sale. Things turned heated, she threw out a few threats, and he laughed at her." She raised her brows and took a sip of her cocoa. "As you can imagine, it did not go well. If he comes down with some strange illness, you'll know who was behind it."

Under the magnifying lens of small-town living, seemingly trivial events sometimes held more significance than an outsider might guess. That was a lesson Clara remembered from the days before the city of Port Harbor swelled and invaded the little hamlet where she was raised. It was funny, she thought, how living among more people allowed for an increased sense of privacy when it seemed just the opposite should hold true.

In an effort to hide a bevy of witches in plain sight, Hagatha rallied them up and formed the Moonstone Circle, an organization that served a combination of civic and social functions while providing a safe space for the coven to meet on the sly.

Scandalized by the idea of a ladies-only club, Pastor Evaniah Johnson prevailed upon some of the members of his flock and once the Brotherhood of Badgers was born, relegated the Moonstones to the status of a ladies' auxiliary group.

Alas, shortly after his tireless efforts to push through the inception of the Badgers and usurp the Moonstones, Evaniah suffered a horrifying affliction. Much to his astonishment, his dangly bits petrified and fell off.

The damage was done, the rivalry cemented, but all the coven would agree it had been a genius plan that allowed them to fly under the radar—literally—until their fearless leader decided she was tired of living in secrecy and wanted to let her witchlight shine for all the world to see.

"If Hagatha ever figures out the coven brought you here to keep her under wraps, she's going to wreak havoc on us all. I swear it's enough to make me want to take up day drinking."

Pfft, Mag thought to herself, *as if there aren't already two fingers of Bailey's in that cup of cocoa.*

"What's wrong with that niece of hers?" Mag said out loud. "Isn't she supposed to keep tabs on old Haggie?"

"Between you and me, that girl is about half a string short of a set of Christmas lights." Even in metaphoric speech, Gertrude's mind ran on a single track.

Mag quoted Gertrude an estimate for the sleigh and dragged Clara out of there, leaving the overgrown elf to decide if she could part with the beloved trinket. They made it just past Gertrude's candy-cane-lined front walkway before she burst into a diatribe.

"As if a thousand-year-old high priestess like Hagatha thinks the Balefire witches moved to town for the sole purpose of peddling antiques and lotions." Mag hmphed. "And goddess love her, but doesn't Gertrude know the holiday season ended months ago? I didn't realize her obsession with Christmas lasted the whole bloody year."

"I'm guessing her recent encounter with Wizard Claus himself has burgeoned her holiday spirit. When summer rolls around, and it's hotter than the blazes, you'll be singing a different tune while you're enjoying snow cones and ice skating at her Christmas-in-July party."

Mag gave her a questioning look.

"Oh, yes, she told me all about it when you disappeared *into the bathroom.*" Clara made air quotes, knowing full well her sister had merely used the calling of nature as an excuse to snoop around Gertrude's second floor. "Penelope Starr agreed to conjure a miniature snow squall in Gertrude's backyard for the occasion."

"Penelope Starr," Mag growled. As much as she hated to admit it, Penelope's conjuration abilities were a tad more developed than her own. Even more galling since there was little doubt the ladder-climbing witch had manipulated her way into taking over the duties of High Priestess while Hagatha was technically still on the job. Worse, she expected the Balefire sisters to do her dirty work and keep the old witch in line.

"Tell me," Clara said, leaning toward her a little, "because I'm dying to know—what's her bedroom like?"

Mag declined to gossip, but she did whistle a popular holiday tune all the way home.

"Say you love me." Clara's familiar, Pyewacket, sing-songed the minute her witch companion stepped over the threshold. Able to shift from cat to human form at will, familiars carried their own brand of magic. Normally, Pye and Jinx served more functions than the ones to which they were being put since moving to a town where hiding one's witchlight was expected. A rule that affected both witches and their lifelong companions.

"I sold that hideously overwrought silver tea service for a tidy profit right after you left, which means you can't even get mad at me for letting Hagatha pinch a few fennel fronds out of the greenhouse."

"Says who?" Mag sputtered. "You know the drill when it comes to Hagatha. Contain and confine. How hard is that to understand?"

"Pfft. Do I look like I'm made out of miracles? When I told her you didn't like people messing around with your plants, she called me a cute little kitten and threatened to turn my tail into a ball of yarn so I would have a new hobby to keep me busy."

Pyewacket arched her back in much the same way she would if in cat form. "If you want Hagatha Crow contained and confined, you'd better invest in a goblin-made cage and troll to stand guard." Ire infused Pye's golden skin with a dull red flush. "And all I did was open the door, Jinx practically carried her into the backyard." Pyewacket threw Mag's familiar so far under the bus he could smell the exhaust.

Jinx let out a nervous giggle that sounded both girlish and desperate to Clara's ears. As different from his witch companion as night is to day, he preferred a sunny corner to the thick of battle. Clara couldn't help thinking his personality, or lack thereof, balanced out against Mag's fiery spirit and willingness to take on the world.

Still, there must be something more to him than suggested by his appearance and demeanor, since Mag's successes as a warrior required the support of a strong companion. Maybe the pale skin and wispy white hair hid a lion-hearted interior, but if they did, Clara had yet to see that side of him.

Clara petted Pyewacket's arm, using the same strokes as she would to soothe a cat. Despite their ability to appear human, familiars were pure feline at heart.

"Powerful things often come in small packages," she said. "You are right to be wary of someone with so much

24

magic and so little impulse control. Don't fret. Mag knows it was our choice to move here, and that the job dangled in front of us came with a cargo-plane-sized load of baggage."

Clara's rebuke, though mildly delivered, hit its target dead center and if Mag didn't exactly apologize, she did let the scowl drop off her face and gave Pye a commiserating smile. "Did you see which way she went when she left?"

Jinx nodded toward the back room, pale face flushing a pink so delicate it wouldn't have looked out of place on a baby bootie knitted by a grandmotherly type.

The shuffle and thump of a tennis-ball-footed walker preceded the creaking comment, "Who said I left?" Entering the room, Hagatha burned Mag with a look.

"He did," Pyewacket jerked a thumb toward Jinx, and then held up both hands in surrender. "You're back, my shift is over. I'm out." Long and lithe, she stalked across to the stairs leading up to Clara's living space, her footsteps turning to the soft shush of paw treads about halfway up the flight.

"I'm...I'll just be..." Stammering, Jinx followed as if his tail was on fire. Or in danger of turning into twisted wool.

In her day—which, according to Mag, must have been somewhere around the same year dirt was invented—Hagatha Crow had been a stunning specimen of a witch. Now, well into the last stages of her crone period, her face looked like the windward side of an old barge—storm-tossed and weathered by time. Amid deeply-etched wrinkles, dark eyes twinkled with intelligence and the fire of mischief. Reports of Hagatha's senility were very much overrated.

Hagatha had long ago used up the last of her give-a-damn and made it her goal not to die until she'd revealed the presence of magic to the world. Or at least to the town of Harmony.

"What were you doing back there, Haggie?" That she had been up to no good was a given, and Clara always had something on the brew in one of the big cauldrons suspended over the hearth where the magical Balefire crackled. Having been born into the family entrusted to tend the flames that fed the source of witch magic, Mag and Clara were Balefire witches in more than surname only.

"Ought to crown you the queen of twisted knickers," Hagatha chortled. A gnarled fist lifted to display one of Clara's sample packets clutched between knob-knuckled fingers. "Thought I'd test the wares, see if this stuff can take ten years off my age."

"Like anyone could tell." Mag didn't even bother to hide the snark.

"Quite a mouth you've got." Admiration edged out the censure in Hagatha's tone as she stuffed the sample packet in with the fennel fronds peeking out of her coat pocket. "You ladies try to be on time tomorrow; we've got a celebration to plan. One this town won't soon forget."

The Moonstones hosted all sorts of functions over the course of every year. Potluck dinners to benefit families in need, a summer program for kids, bake sales, dances, and town-wide celebrations. Despite the Brotherhood of Badger's attempt to take credit for anything that benefited the town, the women of the coven were responsible for revitalizing Harmony and taking advantage of its location to attract tourism. It didn't hurt that Harmony's Founder's Day landed near Memorial Day weekend, the official kickoff of tourist season.

Mag waited until the ancient witch was out of sight and hearing range before she stomped into the back room. Mere seconds passed before she returned. "Whole place reeks of some kind of spell, but since she's so smooth with her magic, I can't tell exactly what she did. Crazy old bat."

Enchanted to double the size of what had once been a cramped storage space, the area behind the curtain, as it were, of Balms and Bygones included a generous workstation where Clara whipped up and packaged her product line. Bottles and jars, after being purified by the flames of the Balefire crackling merrily in the hearth, filled boxes piled under a long, low table. Half a dozen mortar and pestles in various sizes lined one end and a handsome set of antique scales that Mag was dying to put up for sale in the main shop rested nearby.

The packing station boasted funnels, measuring beakers, and rolls of peel-and-stick labels mounted to a shelf above a tall countertop where rested the box of samples Hagatha had raided. Only two of the five cauldrons contained product in some stage of readiness, and Clara focused on those first.

"I'm not taking any chances," she sighed and with a flick of her wrist, winked the cauldrons empty. "Two day's worth of brewing down the tubes. I'll have to start from scratch." Another flick sent a flood of containers flying off the shelves and deposited new ingredients into the sparkling clean, cast-iron pots. "You don't think she got into anything that was sealed, do you? There's at least two months' worth of inventory in here, and I'd hate to lose it all."

"I don't know, Clarie. I'm not sensing hurtful intentions, even if Haggie's mischief knows no bounds. Still, you seal the jars using magic, so that's one bit of protection right there. And you put the best of intentions into everything you brew, so that's another. Probably cast a divining charm to see if she could ferret out your secret recipes."

"Well, she's barking up the wrong tree there, though why she would even care is beyond me." Clara retorted.

"Something tells me she's already marked every tree in the forest. Looks like we'll be needing a little extra protection—Hagatha-specific. I'll see what I can come up with." Mag followed Clara back into the shop.

"Thanks, Maggie. And get rid of those doilies while you're at it. Don't think I didn't notice you sneaking them back into my displays."

Mag stuck out her tongue in an infantile gesture, but she flicked the lacy circles away, at least for the time being. Irritating her sister had become an integral part of Mag's day, and she'd no intention of stopping anytime soon.

Chapter Three

"Get your lazy butt out of bed, Clara Balefire. It was your idea to pick a peck of mugwort at the crack of dawn. Why I'm forced to act as your alarm clock when I've already brewed your coffee is beyond me." Mag's voice trailed off as she stomped back downstairs to the kitchen while Clara rolled her eyes, sighed, and attempted to yank the covers back over her head. Before she could drift back into dreamland, Pyewacket and Jinx pounced on top of her and let out a pair of yowls loud enough to wake the dead.

"I'll ban tuna from the house if you do that again." The familiars knew full well the threat was an empty one, and so they stepped up their game. Flashing into human form, they treated Clara to a duet in perfect harmony of "The Song That Doesn't End."

"All right, all right, I'm up." Clara's fuzzy-sock-clad feet hit the floor with a resounding thump, and with a snap of her fingers, she was dressed to start the day. "Shoo, you two."

When Clara finally descended the stairs, her sister was anxiously tapping her foot against scrubbed-to-gleaming oak floorboards, wearing an irritated expression on her deeply-lined face. Mag ignored Clara's blown raspberry, shoved a thermal mug of hazelnut-scented, caffeine-laden perfection and an empty basket into her hands, and the pair padded out onto the back porch.

"We'll have plenty of time; the sun hasn't even started to crest yet. You'll thank me next time one of your spells calls for mugwort dew, Miss Snarky Pants." Clara teased her sister.

Mag snorted. "There's a first time for everything."

Heaving an exaggerated sigh, Mag leaned more heavily on her cane than necessary, and followed Clara down a cobbled path leading toward the riverbank. When they'd scouted the property the previous winter, a recent thaw followed by a sudden re-freeze had pushed large chunks of broken ice far enough onto the shore that when spring arrived, and the water level returned to normal, it felt like the backyard had doubled in size.

The phenomenon had also disturbed the soil enough to create the perfect conditions for an abundant mugwort harvest, and Clara was determined to take advantage of the blessing. Being able to use the term "locally grown" in the ingredients list for her homemade products was an added bonus.

For all of Mag's griping, she enjoyed walking the trail between her new home and the town square. Not as much as she would enjoy a solo trip across the Andes lost in the wild thrill of the hunt, but that life was over. Time might heal most wounds, but never the ones of its own making, and if she had to be put out to pasture, Harmony's grass was as good as any.

"This is certainly a change, wouldn't you say?" Clara asked as they picked their way along the shore, every now and then finding a patch of feathery, dew-laden greens. With a snip of her shears, Clara clipped off some of the tender plants, shaking the beads of moisture into a wide-mouthed jar before adding the cuttings to the basket.

"I watched the suburbs swallow our home," she said as she sorted through to find the best shoots, "and I thought if I ever got back to myself again, I'd seen enough that it would be easy to acclimate. Twenty-five years frozen in time went by so slowly, but the world moved on, and I still feel like a walnut in an almond shell sometimes. Harmony seems like a nice enough place, and it's good to feel needed and vital after all those idle years."

"You know how I feel about crowds, Clarie," Mag replied. The use of her special pet name for her sister indicated she'd finally softened. "Still, maybe this little adventure of ours won't be so bad after all. I'll get to spend time with you, and watching Hagatha at work is anything but boring. I can see why the coven got tired of dealing with her." Mag accepted another handful of clippings from Clara and placed them in the basket.

"Can't say I blame them for that, but it's a shame nonetheless. I hope when we start to turn senile, we don't get tossed off like an old pair of shoes. Speaking of which..." Distracted by something she saw on the ground, Clara tripped, let out a grunt, and wound up on her backside covered in mugwort clippings, chestnut hair floating around her head in a disheveled halo.

Mag barked out a laugh, only sobering when she noted the expression of shocked consternation on her sister's face as she stared at a pair of shoes protruding from under a leafy bush.

For a fraction of a second, Mag wondered if either the glare from the rising sun or perhaps her old, tired eyes were playing tricks on her before resigning herself to the fact that there were, indeed, feet and legs attached to the shoes.

"I'm afraid we're not in Kansas anymore," Clara said, pushing herself up and taking a closer look at the feet that had tripped her. "Is that what I think it is?"

Clara nodded, "If you think it's a dead body, you'd be correct. What should we do?"

"Well, obviously you need to get out that blasted little contraption of yours and for once put it to good use. Call the cops. And don't touch anything. Forensics will want to sweep the area for trace evidence." Mag said knowingly. "It's procedure for unattended deaths."

Given the gravity of the situation, Clara resisted the urge to point out that Mag's closest dealings with a human forensics team came from her nightly obsession with police and crime shows. Instead, she pulled out her cell phone to do as her sister instructed.

"It's a woman, for sure, but I can't see her face from this angle." Mag crouched into a squat position worthy of the Yoga Journal, her injury forgotten and her cane left lying in the grass at her side. "It looks like she must have fallen and then rolled under there. See how none of the branches of this bush are bent or broken?" Mag pointed to the bridge towering overhead. "I didn't realize we'd come this far already. Tell them to take the footpath from the clock tower; we're not more than a stone's throw from the town square."

Clara relayed the necessary information, and to Mag's surprise, snapped a few photos of the grisly scene.

"What? If you weren't so tech-phobic, you'd be doing the same thing. Besides, you know you'll thank me later because if my intuition is screaming, yours must be whistling Dixie."

Using her cane for extra balance, Mag navigated the rocky hill to get to a position that revealed more of the body.

"Come here and look. I think I know who it is." Her voice held a note of sadness, and Clara scrambled up the bank to stand next to her sister. Leaves concealed the dead woman's face, and the terrain was too steep for them to bend over for a closer look without losing balance, so Clara snapped another series of photos before pocketing the phone.

Paisley cloth in colors now muted by mud and moss stains wrapped around thighs scraped by rough passage over sticks and stones. The bodice, barely visible below where the rest of the body disappeared into the glossy green foliage, was badly torn.

"You recognize that dress, don't you?" Mag asked gravely.

"I do," Clara replied. "Let's say the blessing for the dead, then leave her for the proper authorities, and we'd better make it the short version."

Together they chanted:

Gentle air carry her spirit home.

Mighty fire purify her soul.

Abiding water cleanse her pain.

Mother earth receive her heart.

Blessed   be   until   the   wheel   returns   thee.

Less than five minutes—which felt like at least fifty—later, a rustling noise signaled the approach of two men as they marched down the embankment to where the poor, dead woman lay. The younger of the two, a salt-and-pepper-haired man of about forty-five, clad in a police uniform, looked from Mag to Clara with a suspicious glint in his eyes.

"What were the two of you doing out here at this time of day? I don't know how they do things in the big city, but..." His beer belly jiggled over a large belt buckle in the shape of a ram's head. Neither Mag nor Clara got to hear exactly how things were done in a small town because the second man interrupted the interrogation with a wave of his hand.

"Chief Cobb, I think you can relax. See that basket? I believe these ladies are out here picking...some kind of weed." He reached out and pulled a piece of mugwort out of Clara's hair, his pleasant face turning bright red as his eyes met hers.

"I'm Mayor Norm McCreery, and I don't believe we've been properly introduced. You two recently purchased the old crow's house—I mean, Hagatha Crow's old house. Margaret and Clara Balefire, am I right?" As if Mag didn't exist, he directed his comments to Clara.

"Balefire," he said, tapping his chin and appraising the two women. "Interesting name. I apologize for Chief Cobb's lack of sensitivity. His people skills could use a little work. Ah, here's the EMT crew. Too bad it looks like it's too late for them to do anything."

As is the way of it in many small northeastern towns, people often wear several hats, and one of the emergency technicians conveniently served as the county coroner.

Treating Clara to a crooked smile, the mayor rejoined a scowling Chief Cobb who had finished his preliminary examination and stepped aside to allow the coroner to move the body.

"If you ladies wouldn't mind taking a few steps back," the mayor said, "we'll need to ask you some questions as soon as we're done here."

"The chief is a bit brusque, but Mayor McCreery seems nice," Clara said in a tone low enough that only her sister could hear her.

"Mayor McCreepy if you ask me," Mag muttered under her breath.

"I don't know. He's handsome in that backwoods kind of way. Strikes me as the type of guy who owns a pair of red plaid flannel pajamas."

Mag rolled her eyes, "There's absolutely no reason for you to be imagining that man in his pajamas."

Clara jabbed her with an elbow. "That's not what I meant, and you know it. Get your mind out of the gutter and

34

look—they're pulling her out." Clara jumped to her feet and stepped a few paces closer to the victim, Mag on her heels.

"We were right. It's Marsha from the newspaper office." Clara confirmed unnecessarily since Mag could see that clearly for herself.

The coroner squatted next to the body, looking back over his shoulder to speak to Chief Cobb. "This head wound looks like the cause of death. I'd say she bounced off a rock somewhere before landing here. The preliminary estimate is she's been dead maybe twelve hours, a little less. Between ten and twelve. I'll know more when I get her on the table."

Ten or twelve hours would put the time of death between six and eight o'clock the night before. Just a few hours after the sisters had met Marsha for the first time.

"Seemed like such a nice woman," Clara whispered to Mag. "What a shame. I wonder if she fell, or if she...you know...jumped on purpose."

Mag drew her brows down and huffed. "Don't be stupid. Anyone who's serious about jumping off a bridge doesn't do it so close to the end. You want to die, you go right out into the middle where there's less chance of anything breaking your fall. Maximum velocity."

Clara looked at her like she'd lost her mind. "That's the most morbid thing you've ever said to me. Shh, he's coming back."

Mayor McCreery ambled back over to Mag and Clara. "I'm sorry you had to find her like this. Did you know Marsha Hutchins?"

"No." Clara replied, "I mean, we met her just yesterday at the newspaper office. She seemed nice. Do you know if she—"

"The guardrail on that bridge has been in need of repair since the Lester boys rammed it with their Jeep Wrangler last fall. It looks like Marsha must have been on her way home, stumbled and fell. She was known to take the footpath. Wouldn't be the first time someone has fallen—"

"Well, don't you think, Mr. *Mayor*, that you ought to do something about it?" Mag interrupted without mincing words. It didn't seem to matter to her that perhaps another time and place would have been more appropriate for a conversation about civic duties. Then again, Mag had never been fast friends with Miss Manners.

Mayor McCreery's face flushed a darker red than before. "Well, yes, you're probably right." He turned his attention back to Clara, obviously considering her the more reasonable of the pair. "I assure you, this was nothing more than a tragic accident, but the crime scene team from our county office will follow up. I do apologize. You and your mother have only been in town a few weeks, and I can't imagine how we compare to the way things are run in the city."

"Not at all, Mr. Mayor. Port Harbor isn't the thriving metropolis some people imagine it to be. I'm sure you'll do your due diligence."

"Clarie, I seem to be having another of my episodes," Mag's voice had gone from commanding to breathy in a matter of seconds, and she once again leaned heavily on her cane. Clara quirked an eyebrow but followed through with the necessary niceties before leading her sister slowly up the hill and into town.

Once they were out of sight of the mayor and police chief, Mag's strength returned full-force. "I'd bet my wand hand and a wad of Ben Franklins this was no accident. Couldn't you feel it?"

Clara nodded, glancing over her shoulder. "Something was definitely off, but we shouldn't jump to conclusions."

"I have no intention of jumping in any way, shape, or form. I intend to investigate, and you're going to help me."

36

Mag marched ahead of Clara, who remained pensive as they ascended the hill and wove their way through a maze of gardens adjacent to the town office. Her absentminded admiration of a rainbow of budding tulips was rudely interrupted as the clock tower looming overhead rang out the seven o'clock hour.

"I'm glad we don't live right next door to that thing. We'd both need hearing aids inside of a week. It's loud enough at the house as it is." Clara griped, sticking a finger in her ear and wiggling it around.

"What's that now?" Mag cupped her ear with one hand and grinned.

"You goof. Look, there's Leanne in the newspaper office." Clara pointed and dragged Mag across the grass and onto Main Street. Spurred by the desire to get as far away from the clock bells as possible, she set a brisk pace. "Should we go talk to her?"

Mag squared her shoulders as much as she could, anyway—they remained slightly hunched even when she stood upright—and led the way inside. "Hello, Leanne," she said to the young lady inside. "Do you remember us? I'm Mag, and this is my daughter, Clara."

"Sure, sure, come on in. Marsha should be here any minute. Maybe she slept in because we worked late finalizing the layout last night. Still, It's not like her to be tardy when there's a special edition in the works."

Clara and Mag exchanged a glance that included a silent conversation:

She doesn't know.

We're going to have to tell her.

You do it.

No, you do it.

37

Clara sighed; it was probably best for her to break the news. Gently, as the gravity of the situation warranted. "Leanne, I hate to have to tell you this, but Marsha won't be coming in today. She passed away last night."

Chapter Four

Leanne blinked and looked back and forth between Clara and Mag with the disbelief that follows devastating news. Every ounce of color drained from her face, she mouthed the word *no*, and then promptly burst into tears. "What are you talking about? That can't be true. How?"

"It seems she fell from Spurwink Bridge."

"Are you sure? Maybe it was someone else. A mistake."

"I'm sorry," Clara said, her face kind, "but we were the ones who found her. There's no mistake."

Shaking, Leanne stumbled toward her desk chair, sinking into it as though she could no longer trust her legs to hold her up.

"From the bridge? Oh, no. I've tried telling her not to go that way at night, but she never listens. Listened, I mean. If only…" Leanne's voice shook as she revised her statement to the past tense. Fresh tears ran in tracks down cheeks heavily coated with rouge and full-coverage concealer just a shade too dark for her porcelain complexion. "Was it quick, or did she…you know…suffer?"

Mag shot Clara a pointed look. Basic human interaction was Clara's strong suit, so Mag allowed her to take the reins, and began glancing around the office with narrowed eyes.

"No, I don't believe she did. The police seem to think it happened quickly." Clara had no idea whether the statement was truthful or not, but she knew with complete conviction it was what Leanne needed to hear.

"I'm so sorry," she said as the girl continued to cry. "I didn't realize you two were so close." She fished for information under the guise of concern, the heavy disadvantage of being new in town weighing on her mind.

Once Mag was on the scent of wrong-doing there would be no stopping her. Doggedly, she would insert herself—and Clara by extension—into the investigation until the solution presented itself. Hopping on board was Clara's only option, and the fact that she'd genuinely liked Marsha during their brief meeting provided additional motivation.

"Marsha was the best friend I've had in years. I mean, we had our disagreements, but that's normal. You're family; you must know what I'm talking about."

You couldn't possibly imagine, Clara thought while Mag snorted her agreement from across the room.

"When did you see her last?"

"Yesterday evening, about seven o'clock. When I left, Marsha was trying to install the drivers for that new printer, ranting about not being able to find the model number and cussing out Perry for not answering his phone. But he was coming in just as I was heading out. I yelled at him about the blown bulb in the back room. He's got a key; he could have fixed it anytime." If the initial estimate was correct, Leanne had just narrowed the time of death down by an hour.

"I was in a rush to get home and help put the kids to bed. Dylan is great with them, but he sometimes forgets to make them brush their teeth," she said with a fond but watery smile.

Clara made a mental note to strike up a mock casual conversation with Perry Weatherall the next time opportunity arose, and while she was pondering the implications, an awkward silence fell.

"If you'll excuse me, I need to close up here and go…" Leanne trailed off on a sob and a hard swallow before she pulled herself back together. "I'm sorry. I'm afraid there may be a delay in placing your ad. I'm sure you understand there might not even be a paper after what's happened."

Clara nodded in understanding, "Of course, that's the least of our concern right now."

"Thank you for stopping by and telling me about Marsha. I'll give you a call when things have been properly sorted." Leanne's voice cracked with emotion and it became clear she needed a moment of privacy to process everything she'd just learned.

"Do you mind if I use your restroom first?" Mag pasted on her best *old lady with a weak bladder* face and squeezed her legs together for dramatic effect.

"Sure, it's just through there." Leanne pointed to a door near the rear of the room, the same one that housed the back exit where Perry and Bryer had delivered the printer the day before. "Lock the back door when you let yourselves out, please." Leanne bustled out through the front and, before turning and heading toward the town square, locked that door from the outside.

"Not too bright, is she? Just walking out the door and leaving strangers to mind the store like that."

"Grief makes people do strange things sometimes." Eyes soft with empathy, Clara stood for a moment wondering what would happen to the paper with Marsha no longer at the helm.

"Clarie! Quick, come here." Mag's muffled voice wafted in from the back hallway, interrupting Clara's reverie.

Part storage and part museum of printing history, the back room was jam-packed with bits of leftover things. A hulk of an old printing press squatted in one corner and looked as if all it needed was a bit of oil and a thorough dusting before it would be ready to spark back to life. The sharp scent of ink lingered around the rollers.

Boxes piled high in the corner opposite the press, and the new laser printer stood in the space along the wall in between. More boxes lay under a long table that took up half of the fourth wall, the one to the left of the back door.

"I was right! Look what I found stuck in the door jamb." Mag held up a piece of paisley printed cloth, a perfect match to the dress Marsha had been wearing when she died. Clara brandished her cell phone, flicked at the screen a couple times to pull up the morbid photographs she'd taken of the body, and verified—unnecessarily, as far as Mag was concerned— that the scrap of fabric had been torn from Marsha's bodice.

"You know what this means, don't you? We're standing right in the middle of the scene of the crime!"

"A crime of fashion?" Clara replied dryly.

"And it was most definitely murder." Excited, Mag ignored the comment.

"Technically, we know nothing of the sort. Marsha might have snagged her dress on the door on her way out." Clara replied with caution, always the more level-headed of the two, at least to her mind. Mag tended to see murder and mayhem and conspiracies around every corner.

"If you still don't trust my instincts after two and a half centuries, Clarie, we've got some serious trust issues to work through." Mag sighed, wishing for once her sister didn't think she'd gone off half-cocked. Her body might look an advanced age, but her mind was still sharp as a tack.

Clara mimicked Mag's uneasy inhalation of breath, "I believe there's something wonky going on here, but we have to account for all possibilities. That's all I'm saying."

"Weren't you paying attention to the body? The shape of this scrap matches the torn piece from the bodice of Marsha's dress. Who snags their boobs on a door jamb while exiting a building? She'd have had to bend all the way over, which makes no sense."

"Neither does it being torn during a scuffle. It's an odd position to be in regardless."

"Not if someone carried her," Mag held her arms in front of her, as if cradling a body, "and stepped sideways through the door. She may only have been unconscious at that point. I caught no trace of blood when I scanned the office."

It disturbed Clara to know Mag could sniff out the scent as easily as a bloodhound. Perhaps she'd once again underestimated her sister.

Patting her pockets, Mag pulled out a vial of potion that shimmered all the colors of a sunset and laid it on the table. Fascinated, Clara watched as two more vials and several packets joined the first, along with a twist of knotted string, a stubby black candle, a miniature crystal ball, an amulet, and a chicken foot.

"Gotta hand it to you, you certainly are prepared."

"I'm traveling light these days, but you never know when you might need a few things and if the killer used bleach to clean up after…you know…I could have missed it." The barb of Clara's sarcasm missed its mark as several more items landed on the slick surface. Elbow deep in a pocket that looked to be big enough to hold two nose tissues and a paperclip, and it still didn't seem as though Mag had found the particular item she wanted.

Patiently, if with a smirk, Clara waited and watched.

"I know I have…oh, found it." Mag pulled a packet of folded and sealed waxed paper from the depths and handed it

43

to her sister before methodically returning everything else to her pockets.

"What is it?" Curious, Clara sniffed at the seal.

"Careful with that. It's a mix of pixie dust and powdered bloodstone." Mag took the parcel and whispered an incantation over it where it lay in the flat of her hand. Like a living thing, the paper unfolded.

"Stand back, now." Stepping in front of her sister, Mag applied a light breath to the glinting powder to send sparkling motes streaming into the room. The swirling cloud expanded, spun in place for a few seconds, then arrowed toward the corner of the printing press.

"Bingo." It wasn't quite a cackle, but a delighted laugh all the same. "There's fresh blood trace on the press. Look." Pixie dust particles that looked like multicolored firefly lights blinked in a display that would have seemed merry if not for the fact that they indicated someone had bled there.

After a second, more thorough search turned up no new evidence, Clara pulled Mag out the back exit, diligently locking the door as they went and discussing their theory of the murder.

"This means anyone who had contact with Marsha last night is a suspect. Except for Leanne, I think. Marsha was taller than her by at least a foot. I can't see her having the strength to carry all that dead weight. And we hardly know anyone in town, so getting the information ought to be a piece of cake." Clara rolled her eyes with sorrowful sarcasm.

"You forget, Clarie, that this isn't Port Harbor. Around here, you'll be considered a weirdo if you aren't a Miss Marple-level busybody. I'm sure we'll find out more about Marsha than we ever wanted to know over the next few days—probably even weeks—with the vast majority comprised of conjecture and outright lies."

With a conspiratorial wink, Mag grabbed Clara's coffee cup out of the basket she still carried, dumped the dregs down a nearby sewer grate, and headed for the door of Evelyn's Bakery, "Well, let's see what we can find out, shall we?"

It had taken less than an hour for the news of Marsha's death to reach the insatiable ears of the Harmony public. When anything happens in a small town, all it takes is one fly on the wall to set the rumor mill churning. That one fly whispers softly to her cricket friend, who repeats the information—not, of course, in its entirety—to a little birdie, and on down the grapevine it travels until all the buzzing and chirping is nothing more than background noise.

Unfortunately, the unlucky SOB occupying the bottom branch of the phone tree is like the last person at the end of a long game of Telephone, and what she hears usually bears little resemblance to the original statement.

"Looks like we came to the right place. Half the town is crammed in here," Mag's eyes lit up as she surveyed the establishment, which could hardly be described as just a bakery.

The original Evelyn had focused her immeasurable talents on creating the fluffiest, most delicious glazed donuts known to mankind, but her daughter, the current reigning Evelyn, had jumped on board the coffee and cafe train right around the time Harmony had vetoed the addition of a Starbucks. She went from serving just donuts to providing a variety of breakfast items, plus soup and sandwiches at lunchtime.

"Go find us a seat, if you can. You want your usual?" Clara asked.

"No, make it Mint Delight today; wintergreen helps me think more clearly," Mag replied.

Clara snorted, considered her sister's request, and ordered one for herself as well.

45

"What a shame, she was such a lovely woman." A customer Clara only vaguely recognized shook her head sadly while waiting for her order.

Mrs. Green, an elderly neighbor of Mag and Clara's, clucked in agreement while she poured copious amounts of sugar into her coffee cup, throwing caution and concern for dietary restrictions out along with the paper wrappers, "Maybe it was a blessing, after all, that she never had any children. These young'uns and their need for a career these days, I tell you…"

Clara exchanged a small smile with Evelyn, who she judged to be about the same age as Marsha—no more than thirty-five if Clara's instincts were on point—while Mrs. Green launched into a diatribe on her views regarding modern-day women.

Fortunately, Evelyn understood that the phrase "the customer is always right" often requires a solid metric- ton of patience, and a willingness to part ways with your own opinions once the sign on the door flips to the "open" side.

By the time she made it to the table where Mag huddled, Clara had heard the name Marsha whispered in reverent tones at least three times.

"They barely moved the body yet, and already everyone in town knows what happened." Clara's statement held no measure of surprise; it was to be expected.

Mag examined the faces in the shop, thinking. "Yes, and the display of false sympathy is positively shameful. Nobody is universally loved, especially not someone like Marsha."

"What do you mean?" Clara aimed a quizzically raised eyebrow at her sister.

"She wasn't a pushover, that's what I mean."

"You got that out of watching her in action for half an hour?"

46

"Sure did. The woman had a spine. Didn't you see that? Strong women are never popular—powerful, yes, but they're not always well liked. Could be what got her killed."

"Shh, Mag, or you'll whip the whole town into a frenzy." Clara admonished as her sister's voice steadily increased in volume. "Let's go, we're not going to find out anything useful right now. Not until the shock dissipates and people stop eulogizing her."

On their way out the door, Clara tripped over the threshold and nearly did Hagatha's job for her as instinct and self-preservation had her conjuring a spell to keep herself from nosediving into the sidewalk. Thankfully, steady arms caught her mid-fall, and when she had been put to rights, Clara found herself looking into the speculative eyes of Bryer Mack.

"Whoa there," He smiled, his voice taking on a husky quality that made Clara's cheeks redden for the second time that day. "Are you okay?"

Bryer's hands were still around her waist, and the scent of his cologne surrounded her like a cloud. Clara disentangled herself with an awkward shake that did more to intrigue than repel him.

"I'm fine. Thank you," she said, running a hand down her front to straighten her clothing.

"I hear you had quite the shock this morning." Bryer's voice held concern and something else—curiosity if Clara wasn't mistaken. *Even the men in this town are insatiable gossipmongers.* She thought uncharitably.

"Yes, we certainly did. Such a tragedy." She mimicked the sentiments circling Evelyn's Bakery. "You were her friend, weren't you? I'm sorry for your loss."

Bryer's face clouded. "It's a tragedy, yes. But I wouldn't call us friends, exactly. We had a professional relationship, but Marsha wasn't close to many people in town, except for

47

Leanne. Not that you'd be able to tell, the way they bickered. Then again, Marsha bickered with just about everyone."

"I'm surprised to hear that. I thought Marsha seemed quite pleasant, and everyone we've talked to this morning has had nothing but nice things to say about her."

"Well, of course, they do. Now." Bryer seemed to agree with Mag's earlier sentiment about glorifying the dead. She inclined her head to indicate Clara should keep him talking.

Clara batted her eyelashes just enough to draw Bryer's attention and murmured a breathy, "How interesting," before lowering her lashes shamefully. "Oh, you must think I'm just the Nosiest Nelly in town."

Bryer seemed to buy her false remorse, hook, line, and sinker. "Not at all. It's only natural. Just ask Perry Weatherall how much of a thorn in the side Marsha could be. Not that I think he'll be happy to learn of her…um…accident. But those two went round and round over the lease agreement for the newspaper office, and he made no bones about his feelings toward Marsha. Personally, I thought she did a bang-up job at the paper, and for that, she'll most definitely be missed."

"Why would Perry Weatherall have a say in Marsha's lease agreement?"

"Oh, Mr. Moneybags bought the entire building, so now he owns roughly a quarter of the town's real estate. I can't complain; he cares about local business, and his dealings have netted me a tidy profit."

Clara, realizing the conversation was coming to a close, gave Bryer an easy out. "Yes, well, so it seems. It was nice to see you. Thanks again for saving me."

"It was my pleasure. You and your mother have a lovely day."

It was all Clara could do to keep a straight face at Mag's barely-contained scowl. "Yes, you too."

"Are you wearing beer-scented perfume today or something?" Mag asked once Bryer had ambled back down Main Street.

"What are you talking about?"

"You know good and well what I'm referring to. That's the second man you've had at your disposal in as many hours." Mag's tone was light and teasing, but deep down the little green monster stirred. She put on a brave face but underneath the tired old facade lurked a woman who, in witch years, should have been in her prime, and it rankled.

"He's too young for me anyway." Clara rolled her eyes.

"Clarie, you have two centuries on every man in town whose hormones are still active, so what difference does a couple decades in appearance make?"

Clara sighed, "I can't explain it. And besides, I have no interest in dating. Period. I've got you and Pyewacket, and that's all the companionship I'm looking for at the moment." Her brusque tone brooked no argument and, considering there were more important things to focus on, Mag let the subject drop.

"At least we found out one tiny tidbit of useful information. Perry Weatherall had full access, and a key to the crime scene."

Chapter Five

"I don't know how I let you talk me into spending my twilight years in this backwater place." Swinging her cane and moving along at a fast clip, Mag spoke over her shoulder and ignored the fact she'd been expounding on the virtues of small-town living, not a day before.

"Excuse me?" Clara said, brows raised and hands on her hips. "*I* talked *you* into moving here? Puh-lease. Let's move to the country, you said. This coven needs us, you said. We can start over somewhere we can make a difference, you said. How is it my fault the job comes with social obligations? No one's asking you to actually attend the festivities. In fact, all you really have to do is sit there and try not to look like there's a burr under your butt. And don't get me started on the *twilight years* thing."

All teasing aside, Clara considered the perfectly valid reasons her sister preferred avoiding most forms of social interaction. Still, she hoped the decision to move wasn't going to become an ongoing argument.

"I'm sorry. Maggie, please." Catching up, Clara gently pulled Mag to a stop, led her to one of the benches in front of the veterans' memorial and, checking to make certain no one was around, used a hint of power to drop a sound barrier that would keep their conversation private. "Are you having second thoughts about all of this? About moving here, becoming a shopkeeper, taking part in an active coven after so many solitary years? Or is it that everyone in town thinks you're my mother?"

"Don't be daft. I'm used to my outside not looking like my inside, and I don't give a damn if people think I use this"—Mag waved the cane she habitually carried—"because I'm old and decrepit. Lulls them into a false sense of security." The statement was true at least ninety-nine percent of the time.

Clara stared at her for a few long seconds, trying to determine the truth of the statement. "How's the leg? You're doing your exercises and using the cream I made for you, right? Sorry, I didn't mean to turn into a mother hen."

She fell quiet for a few seconds, waiting for Mag to answer. When she didn't, Clara blurted, "then what is it? Every witch in that coven knows the story of Margaret Balefire, mighty Raythe hunter. They practically hang on your every word." To her credit, sincerity rang through Clara's tone; she was proud of her sister. Always had been.

"I don't care about me, Clarie. I see how some of them look at you when they think you won't notice. Like you got away with something."

"That? Can you blame them? I was turned to stone, for Hecate's sake. Harm none, that's our way. There's only one immediately punishable offense—witch murdering witch— and one sentence: being turned to stone. I didn't do the former, but I certainly managed the latter. Never mind that it wasn't a true stoning, it looked that way from the outside." She shrugged. "What else would they think when they see me here and in the flesh, so to speak? I was stoned, and now I'm not."

"Which you've explained, and still they look." Mag's vehemence warmed Clara's heart.

"People will believe whatever they want to believe, and there's nothing I can do to change the situation, but I refuse to

51

let anyone's opinion define me." She paused for a few heartbeats to watch a couple stroll by, happily engrossed in each other.

"Let them look," she continued. "We're Balefire witches; some of the strongest in our line, and that alone is enough to draw attention. My daughter hooked up with Cupid and gave birth to a powerful Fate Weaver. It just adds to the mystique. Our exploits are legendary. I'll own that if you will. I choose not to care what they think of me. Or not much anyway. Besides, we're businesswomen now, and you need to present your best face to the community."

Margaret rounded and presented her annoyed face to her sister.

"Not that one! We don't want to scare away customers. Word of mouth travels fast in places like this. You don't want to be known as the new Hagatha, do you? How hard can it be to plan decorations for a dance? I doubt we'll even be called on to offer an opinion since we're new in town. Plus, Hagatha is expecting us, and I'd rather not be cursed by the whackadoodle witch of the east for being excessively tardy. We're already late."

"Can't be any worse than that toilet paper float we're going to be riding on, and thank you for volunteering me for that duty, by the way." Arms linked, the sisters strolled toward the meeting room, Mag complaining with every step.

"It's not toilet paper, it's tissue paper. There's a difference."

"Not much of one."

Clara was spared any more discussion on the matter when they reached their destination. She paused just inside the door as Hagatha's rusty voice soared above the din.

Leaning toward Mag's ear, Clara announced, "Not it," then made a beeline for the end of the hall farthest away from where Hagatha held court, leaving her glowering sister to handle the elderly witch alone.

Did she feel the tiniest bit remorseful about deserting Mag that way? No, Clara decided she did not.

Minding just about the oldest witch on the planet was hard enough, but when said witch had decided the world was ready to know about magic and had recently mounted a one-woman crusade to drag her kind out of the closet, the job turned into a nightmare.

"Did you hear the news?" Gertrude, bedecked in red and green stripes from head to toe, sidled up and whispered in Clara's direction. "That nice woman from the newspaper was found dead yesterday. Marsha Something-or-other. What a shame." Some members of the witch community maintained a healthy distance from the rest of the town. "Word is they've closed up the office, and there won't be a paper at all for the foreseeable future."

"How well did you know her?" Might as well take advantage of the opportunity to learn more about Marsha, Clara thought. Funny how no one seemed to know the Balefire women had found the body. News like that should have gone around town faster than a racehorse could run.

"Oh, I only met her once or twice. Safer to stay away from people who ask questions, you know, when you have secrets to protect. It takes a prying mind to run a newspaper. She came around to do interviews with the group a time or two. Once when we were running a function. Quite nosy with all her questions, she was. But nice. I don't want you to think I'm speaking ill of the dead."

"Did she have family in the area? Was she married?"

"No. No family—or none that I know of since her granddaddy passed away. The family wasn't from around here, to begin with. Can't say I know what happened to her folks, but she was just a babe when the old man moved to

53

town. She grew up, moved away like most of the younger generation does. Why I think she only came back to run the paper about ten years ago. They were newcomers, you see. So I don't know much about the family."

Typical New England mindset. Anyone who didn't come over on a ship named for a Spanish woman or a spring bloom earned the newcomer designation, and as such, landed on a watch list. Of course, Gertrude was a five-hundred-year-old witch. To her, anything under a century would seem like a short time indeed.

"The police ruled it an accident, but people are saying she might have jumped." Gertrude's voice dropped to a whisper. "On purpose."

"Why? Is there a reason she might want to kill herself?"

Gertrude shrugged. "All I know is there's talk. And, in this town, where there's talk, it's because someone has a story they don't want to tell, so they let it out in rumors. Some say it was financial trouble, some say she was sick or something."

"She looked perfectly healthy to me, but you never know nowadays." Clara quickly rejected the idea, her intuition screaming that if Marsha had intentionally ended her life, she'd have made preparations or at least left a suicide note.

"I heard Perry Weatherall tossed her off the bridge so he could break the lease on her office space, but that's just ridiculous," Gertrude continued. "I'd bet it was an affair gone wrong. She was a looker, so that's the most likely reason. Tragic, really. I wonder who it was. There aren't too many eligible men of an age around here."

Clara couldn't swear to it, but she thought Gertrude seemed a little disappointed by that particular sentiment.

"There's Harold Fishman what owns the grocery store, but last I heard, he was stepping out with Sheila Matson. Besides, he's kind of a damp squib between the sheets. I can't see anyone getting riled up enough to commit suicide over him. Never saw her look twice at Norm McCreery, and I know for sure it wasn't Perry Weatherall. The whole town knows those two hated each other. Maybe she was catting around with a married man. That makes more sense."

It was all Clara could do to stop her mouth from dropping open in shock while she listened to Gertrude go from speculation to certainty that Marsha brought about her own demise after being overcome with grief at the ending of a clandestine relationship.

Character assassination, pure and simple, Clara thought to herself. And not a word of it factual given what she and Mag had learned of the crime. Even without confirmation, her sister had recognized it for murder and Clara would put Mag's gut feelings up against Sherlock Holmes's powers of deduction any day of the week.

Poor Marsha. Posthumously condemned to knowing winks and the product of sly, wagging tongues, and all the while, no one would know she was the victim of a brutal murder. The injustice of it burned a hole nearly through Clara. No one should have to die and then be painted with the brush of scandal. As suddenly as it began, the burn in her gut turned to cold determination.

For twenty-five long years, Clara had stood frozen in stone while members of her coven came to confess their sins at the feet of the one witch they knew had done something much worse. All that time, the Balefire name was dragged through the mud over a crime she didn't commit. Marsha being condemned through gossip brought back many of the emotions Clara recognized from her own ordeal.

Hot blood rose up to prickle across her skin, pushing her to act because Marsha's death must be avenged. The poor woman's name must be cleared, and the culprit must not escape punishment. Was this how Mag had felt during her hunting days? No wonder she'd continued and not counted the cost of her thirst for justice.

On the other side of the room, Mag needed no urging to come to a similar conclusion. Murderers or rogue magical beings—it all amounted to the same. Harm an innocent, and you'd have Margaret Balefire to deal with.

The decision was cemented when she listened to one coven member say to another, "You heard about the scandal in New York, right? Cost her that fancy job, and it's the only reason she ended up back here in the first place. Now, this? You just never know about people, do you?"

Whispered innuendo carried the day and turned Mag's face sour with displeasure. Towing Hagatha along for the ride, she made her way back to Clara's side, but before the sisters had a chance to compare notes, Penelope Starr shot her nose in the air and lifted her voice to be heard.

"Ladies!" She clapped her hands. "If you please, it's time to start waving your wands. We need three hundred flowers finished by the time the men show up and we're down to half an hour before that happens."

Sharing the space with "normals" meant a fair amount of caution must be exercised to keep the coven's witchy ways a secret.

"This town event coincides with the Wind Moon celebration, so let's all remember to incorporate the proper elements into your decorations. You do know what you're doing, right?" Penelope Starr, Hagatha's self-appointed successor as high priestess (only because Gertrude herself had vehemently refused the title), hadn't the grace to wait until the post was available before she considered it filled. Maybe she assumed her position as head of the Moonstones made her uniquely qualified.

In her capacity as Circle leader, Penelope surveyed the room from the head of the table where she leaned forward on her palms and pressed her forearms together in an attempt to rival Gertrude's considerable bosom. When her eye landed on Mag's mutinous expression, one eyebrow lifted and her mouth curved into a smirk.

Once past their twenty-fifth birthday, witches enjoyed the benefits of decelerated aging and a greatly expanded lifespan—Clara and Mag were still considered relatively youthful after clocking in over two and a half centuries, even if Clara was the only one of the two who exemplified the phenomenon.

A goodly chunk of Mag's youthful appearance had been siphoned off by the Raythes she'd battled selflessly. Her aged countenance was a mark of great sacrifice—one Penelope refused to acknowledge with proper reverence and respect. She had already made her feelings about the coven's new additions perfectly clear.

Penelope considered the Balefire sisters an unnecessary addition to the coven, and she would have kicked Hagatha out on her wrinkled butt years ago if she wasn't petrified of the karmic kickback. If she had a lick of sense, Penelope would have been more worried about the wrath of Hagatha than by knowing whatever magic she sent out into the world would come back to her times three. Hagatha didn't need the multiplication factor; she could take Penelope out in one fell swoop.

Then again, maybe Penelope figured she could toss one of her two henchwomen in front of her as a shield. Neither Mabel Youngblood nor Evanora Dupree was bright enough to avoid the karma bus before it ran them over.

Mag couldn't stand any one of the trio, referring to them as the "witchy bitches," and Clara found their apparent fixation with attempting to live reality television lifestyles a bit too juvenile for her tastes. The Real Witches of Harmony did NOT have a nice ring to it.

Still, the Circle was a mid-level contributor to half a dozen local charities, and the sharing of a mutual goal had only strengthened the camaraderie of the Harmony coven. Penelope and her minions must have had some redeeming qualities if they could run the Moonstones from inside the coven without getting too far on Hagatha's bad side while keeping the organization's true purpose hidden from the regular humans who made up the majority of the town population. At least, Clara hoped they did. Otherwise, her new lifestyle would get tedious in no time flat.

In response to Penelope's demand, Mag whipped out her wand and flicked it in the general direction of the table. With a stoic face below a single raised eyebrow, she rained a waterfall of tissue-paper flowers over its surface before turning on her heel and returning to the kitchen with a spring in her wobbly step.

"Well, that's more like it." Penelope grudgingly admitted.

Left standing next to Clara, Hagatha chortled and muttered under her breath, "Gonna be a party no one will ever forget." Her posture seemed more hunched than usual, and Clara thought the old witch had something cradled under the argyle-patterned cardigan hanging off her frail shoulders.

"Are you planning something, old mother?" A term of respect between witches.

"No more than usual. Just trying to do something nice for the town. Make the celebration special." Clara wasn't buying Hagatha's innocent facade, but with no evidence of wrongdoing, pursuing the matter wouldn't be that far off from sniffing around the lid of Pandora's box.

On impulse, she turned to Hagatha and asked, "Do you know anything about the death of the newspaper editor?"

"Been listening to gossip, have you? I know she didn't kill herself and she wasn't having an affair with a married man."

"I didn't think so." But Clara found herself talking to thin air. Hagatha had left the building.

Dragging Mag into a dark corner, Clara followed suit, magically reappearing inside the empty Balms and Bygones.

"We're not supposed to skim from the center, and you know it." Mag grinned.

"No one was looking, and I'd had enough of the place to last me a week. Did you hear some of the things Gertrude said about Marsha? The poor woman is lying cold on a slab in the morgue, and they're gossiping about her."

"Did you think human nature had changed all that much while you were out of commission? I'm here to tell you it hasn't. If anything, it's worse. I remember when—"

Clara waved her off. "Don't let's get started on a discussion of the good old days. The only reason there was less gossip when we were young is because there were fewer people, and they weren't connected by phone lines. But people have always been titillated by scandal, so I suppose I should have seen it coming."

Free to work magic in her own home, Clara concentrated for a second and changed her outfit for something comfier. At the flick of her fingers, a tea cart rolled in from the kitchen, steam from the antique floral pot wafting along in its wake.

"That looks like the Windsor that came in on my last shipment. Did you lift it from the inventory?"

"Considering your last shipment came in from the family section of Shadow Hold—"the hidden archive where witches banished unwanted things or items too powerful to be loose in the world—"it's as much mine as it is yours, and you never asked if I wanted to sell it."

Her shrug acknowledging both statements as truth, Mag let it go, accepting the proffered tea and a delicate pink macaroon.

"No one else is looking, you know," Clara said.

"Fine, then I'll take two." Another of the airy treats landed on Mag's plate.

"I didn't mean that. I meant for Marsha's killer. The police have already ruled it an accidental death."

"That might be my fault." From her pocket, Mag pulled a scrap of paisley cloth. "I forgot to put this back, and it was the only clue."

"What about the blood on the printing press? Wouldn't that have shown up if they'd gone looking for it?"

Mag had the grace to seem chagrined. "It would have if I hadn't used the pixie dust on it."

"You tampered with evidence?"

"Just a little bit."

"Then we have to find Marsha's killer. We're the only ones who can."

Chapter Six

Three times, the middle-aged couple gawked in the window but passed by the shop, and Mag all but smelled the curiosity on them.

"Come in. You know you want to." She stopped short of sending out a flickering tongue of magic to lure them inside, but only because she and Clara had agreed never to enhance their business by working on the free will of others. But, oh boy, was she ever tempted.

It wouldn't take much to nudge them into that all-important first step, and once she had them inside, she'd find the one thing they couldn't live without. A bit of silver, maybe, or an occasional table.

Well, there was more than one way to lure a live one. "Pyewacket, could you come down to the storeroom, please?"

When Margaret Balefire said please and in that butter-wouldn't-melt tone besides, Pye knew something was afoot. Since curiosity and cats are natural companions, she made her way down to find out what.

"Human form, if you don't mind."

In a flurry, tawny fur turned to golden skin.

"There's a couple of lookie-loos outside. I want you to show off your excellent badonkadonk," even after several months of trying, Mag had not found the source of the no-cussing charm Hagatha had laid on the house, and it gave her no end of annoyance to have her words turned as they left her mouth. "Tootie fruity…backside—close enough—to that man out there and give him a good a reason to drag his wife inside."

"That's dirty pool isn't it?" Not that Pye cared as long as it didn't get her in trouble with her witch companion, and Clara had never warned her about this type of interference.

"I agreed not to cast any of my charms on the customers, but I never said a thing about not casting yours. Go out there and bend over or something."

Mag's ploy worked well enough; the couple came in just ahead of a local woman who scanned the shelves and made a grab for a tube of skin cream.

"I'm on my lunch break, so if you could ring me up quickly, that would be awesome. Feel my face." She turned to the female half of the reluctant couple, "No really, feel it. I'm telling you, it's as soft as a ripe peach. You've got to try this cream. It's like magic."

A grinning Pye took the money the enthusiastic woman practically tossed at her, and before there was time to make change, the door swung shut behind her.

"I'll have one of those, please," said the Mrs. while her husband locked eyes on a set of Bavarian beer steins. Mag sold him the steins, and that was just the beginning. By the time they left, the couple had parted with several hundred dollars, which put Mag into a good mood.

A good mood that lasted right up until Clara declared it was time to leave for the Moonstone Circle's final party-planning meeting.

Small towns are notorious for throwing celebrations to commemorate even the tiniest of accomplishments. Take the upcoming event, for example. While the Balefire sisters couldn't argue that the money raised during the Founder's Day Festival would go to a good cause—restoring Harmony's decrepit covered bridge—the irony of the situation didn't escape either of them. Ten years prior, the clock tower revamp had coincided with the town's annual birthday celebration, and now the anniversary of one restoration would serve to fund another.

"Next thing you know, we're going to be throwing a shindig on the anniversary of the day they re-roofed the library, or the time the Clemson's dog peed on the red fire hydrant instead of the yellow one. This is ludicrous." Mag griped, pulling on a burnt-orange blouse over a neon-green tie-dyed skirt.

Clara raised an eyebrow at her sister's choice of ensemble, but let the matter drop, knowing full well she'd get an earful about how the nineteen seventies were the epitome of high fashion. She could quote Mag's diatribe word for word and figured if she ever wanted to wear her own favorite eighties-throwback, triangle-print dress—complete with shoulder pads—again without setting off a response, she'd better keep her mouth shut.

"Yes," Clara agreed as her hair magically flipped through several styles until finally settling on a high ponytail. "I know it seems a bit odd, but if you'll recall, we attended a parrot's birthday party back in Port Harbor—and bought a gift, to boot. Besides, this gives us a chance to ferret out some information. I say we hop on board."

"Speaking of ferrets, remember when Delia Slatterhorn made us come to little Kiki's wake?"

"How could I forget? The neighbor's oversized beagle wrenched the carcass right out of the coffin—hand-built, by

63

the way—and took off at a sprint. Poor Delia. Do you remember the look on her face?" Clara let loose an inappropriate laugh and quickly covered her mouth with her hand. "I'm a terrible person. She really loved that ferret, and he was a cute little thing."

"Relax, Clarie, old Delia can't hear you, and I know for a fact not all the tears that day were of sorrow over the tragic loss. Let's go. We've got a murderer to catch."

Harmony's modest town square buzzed with activity as Mag and Clara steeled themselves against the impending onslaught of one Penelope Starr. Having had the foresight to see that Hagatha was, for once, safely ensconced with her niece, Penelope attempted to settle into her role of wannabe High Priestess with gusto.

"Now Perry, you can't possibly expect women of such delicate constitution to sit out in the sun all day, can you?" Penelope drawled, batting her eyelashes in a coquettish manner. "Surely a man as handsome as you, and with such…talents…can find a few more canopies *somewhere*."

Coffee nearly spewed out of Clara's nose at Mag's muttered comment, "Who does she think she is, Scarlett O'Hara? For the love of tiny pickles, that woman is worse than old Haggie by a mile."

"Penelope could conjure up a three-ring circus if she wanted one, to say nothing about a few tents. But, apparently, presenting her heavily-glamoured butt to all the eligible men in town is more fun."

Clara stifled another giggle as Perry attempted to disentangle himself from Penelope's razor-sharp talons. "At least she's not casting right here in the square during broad daylight, like someone else we know would."

"Too true," Mag murmured. Seeing her chance to ask the man a few pointed questions about his purportedly bad relationship with Marsha Hutchins, she marched straight up to

64

Perry without a glance in Penelope's direction. "Hello, Perry, can I bend your ear for a moment?"

Jumping at the chance to exit an uncomfortable conversation, Perry nodded and tossed a hasty *talk to you later* toward Penelope, who glared at Mag and then at Clara before whirling on her heel and stalking off in the opposite direction. Her shrill voice rose above the din, beckoning her entourage to her side.

"Thanks for saving me. That woman is like a leech when she wants something." Perry's shoulders had stopped hovering around his ears, and he looked measurably more relaxed as he ambled across the expanse of grass between the town hall and the bank of shops surrounding the newspaper office. "I owe you one."

A little husky through the middle and with a hairline that looked to be creeping north, Perry's blue eyes and sunny smile had probably left a broken heart or two in his wake.

Mag shot a mischievous grin at Clara, which her sister understood meant that was exactly the position in which she'd wanted Perry Weatherall to find himself: in their debt.

"Looks like the event will go off without a hitch. Perfect timing, too. The town could sure use a happy occasion, considering the pall that's fallen since Marsha Hutchins's death." Mag commented innocently while leaning heavily on her cane.

Perry's eyes clouded over, and the tension returned to his shoulders. "Yes, you're absolutely right. Such a tragedy, and for someone with so much life ahead of her." His voice roughened with emotion, but Perry covered it with a cough. "Bunch of idiots have been spreading rumors. Don't you believe a word of that nonsense. She fell, plain and simple, just like the police report says. Marsha had too much going for her to waste it all by jumping off a bridge. Suicide wasn't in her nature."

65

"You two were close then? Word around town is that you and Marsha had a turbulent relationship." Mag prodded without a trace of remorse. "Something about a disagreement regarding the paper's lease of your building. Maybe you'd know if there's any truth to the story she was having a torrid relationship with an unavailable man."

Perry's head snapped up from where his eyes had been trained on the grass below, and his voice was razor sharp when he exclaimed, "That's not true. Who said that?" He reined it in, appeared to calm down a notch, and shook his head.

"I can't tell you much about her personal life, but that doesn't sound like Marsha. And yes, we had our differences, but that lease-agreement business hasn't been a factor for some time. In fact, I'd just updated the high-speed Internet and donated a gently-used industrial printer to the newspaper so she could do everything in-house."

"Is that why you stopped by the newspaper office the night of her death?" Mag's seemingly innocent question hung in the air while Perry's eyebrows wrinkled together, giving the impression that a fuzzy caterpillar had decided to take a lazy nap on the lower part of his forehead.

Perry's gaze shifted once more to the building across the square, and Clara didn't miss the way his face went carefully blank, "If someone says they saw me there, they were mistaken. The last time I saw Marsha, she was playing beat-the-clock to get the layout done on time. She didn't want to try out the new printer on the special edition in case there was a glitch. Maybe if I had been there…"

Eyes kindling to a blaze, he growled, "Where did you come by that piece of misinformation? Never mind. I'm sure I can guess. Leanne Snow, right? Loves to gossip and has zero grasp on the facts, which is perfectly appropriate for someone who works at a newspaper. Takes her glasses off, forgets where she puts them and fumbles around in a half-blind stupor hunting for them."

"For someone who didn't know the dead woman very well, you seem to know a lot about her."

Perry's face practically iced over and matched his clipped tone, "Good day, ladies."

"Touchy, isn't he?" Mag said, knitting her brow as he stormed off. "He's hiding something; let's put him in the maybe pile."

"You think so?" Clara frowned. "I thought he felt genuinely sorry for Marsha."

Mag opened her mouth to issue a tart rebuttal when a furtive movement drew her attention and forced all thought of Perry Weatherall out of her head.

"Hey, isn't she supposed to be on lockdown for the day?" Mag's gaze landed on Hagatha, who cast a furtive look back over her shoulder before scuttling around the corner of the shady side of the clock tower. "I know we should go roust her and find out what plot she's trying to hatch, but I don't have the gumption to deal with her right now."

"To tell you the truth, I think it's almost easier cleaning up after one of her messes than getting in front of her when she's in the thick of it all. My memory-charm skills have never been better. I might regret saying this, but Hagatha who?"

"Right you are. I saw nothing." Mag agreed.

Chapter Seven

"I don't want to go," Mag insisted.

"Haven't you ever watched a single crime show?" Clara looked at her as if she was explaining something to a simpleton. "The perp always goes to the funeral. If we're at the spot, one of us might pick up a vibe from the killer."

Mag scowled. "I know all that. What I don't understand is why you're making me wear this ugly black dress. It looks like a trash bag and a tablecloth had a wild affair and gave birth to the dark spawn of fashion."

"It's not that bad." Clara took a closer look at her sister. "You're wearing it backward."

"See, it's so ugly I can't tell the front from the back. I look like a reject from a nursing home."

"Quit complaining." Having had enough, Clara dipped into the ball of magic that lay like fire in her belly and cast that power in an arc toward the offending garment. Before Mag had time to say tie-dye, the dress spun the right way around, cinched itself in to fit properly under the arms and around the bust, and the color softened to a deep, velvety green. The skirt shrank to swirl and brush halfway down Mag's calf.

"There, Cinderella, you're ready for the ball. Now get a move on because we're not driving to the cemetery and if you don't hurry up, we're going to be late."

"I'll go, but I'm getting ice cream after it's over."

Shaking her head, Clara led the way downstairs and out the door.

"There you are, Ms. Balefire. I was hoping to run into you today." Norm McCreery separated from the cluster of mourners and hastened toward the Balefire sisters. His gaze swept down over Clara's form and quickly back up to her eyes. His face tinged with red when he saw the quirk of her lips that said she'd noticed his appreciation.

"Please, just call me Clara, Mayor McCreery." The false note of graciousness Clare felt necessary when dealing with the Mayor had Mag muttering insults under her breath.

"And you can call me Norm." To Clara's surprise, the florid little man pulled one of the sample tubes of her soothing oatmeal skin cream out of his shirt pocket. He glanced nervously around to make sure no one was within hearing distance. "You wouldn't happen to have a spare tube, would you? I ran out this morning, and I can already feel my face starting to dry out."

"No, I don't, not on me. This isn't really the appropriate venue for selling product." Her nod indicated the series of gray and white marble monuments to the dead, and the casket suspended over a draped hole. "We're here to pay our respects to Marsha."

"Oh, come on. You've got to help me out here. I need it, you know." The mayor twitched like an addict in dire need of a fix. "Another sample. Anything."

What on earth was wrong with the man? His skin looked perfectly fine. Mag's elbow dug into Clara's ribs hard enough to leave a mark and then it hit them both at the same time.

69

Hagatha.

She snatched the sample from McCreery's hand, held it out of sight, and played a shimmer of Balefire over the plastic. The skin of flame turned purple and winked out, leaving a thin layer of smoke hovering over her palm, which Mag inhaled.

"Compulsion spell," She whispered once she identified the flavor. This was serious business. "A strong one."

Tucking her own elbows in to make sure a second assault on her tender side wouldn't be forthcoming, Clara risked enough magic in public to call a fresh tube into her pocket via a trip through the Balefire to make sure the cream was free of any undue magical influence.

"Oh, my mistake, look what's right here in my pocket. Here, it's on the house." The minute his hand closed over the tube, Norm's face relaxed from anxious to slightly confused. He held up his hand, and to make matters worse, observed its contents as though he'd never seen the container of skin cream before.

"Um, thank you." He shook off the daze and with a puzzled, sidelong glance at Clara, then found someplace else to be.

"I'm going to kill her. Being stoned won't be so bad. You can put me in a garden where there are pretty flowers and birds, and it will all be worth it." Mag searched the area for a glimpse of the stoop-shouldered old witch.

"It could have been worse," Clara's observation netted her a snort from Mag as she held out her hand for the bespelled tube. "Feels like it was a one-off spell. How many of these samples do you think we've handed out this week?"

"Thirty, maybe forty. I think half the box was gone when Jinx helped me get those silver candlesticks down from the top shelf this morning. Pye's been dropping the tubes in every bag, and we've handed them out like candy."

Pulling out her phone, Clara sent her fingers flying over the touch-screen to warn Pye about the possible onslaught, and instructed her to toss the rest of the box into the Balefire's purifying flames. "I guess I know what I'll be doing for the next few days: replacing the sample stock, and now that we've isolated the flavor of her spell, clearing the storeroom of every last vestige."

Spring rains had left the ground soft enough to dig Marsha's grave and also to make for a muddy walk to the service.

Tight-faced with grief, mourners clustered on either side of the royal blue casket topped with a blanket of red roses. *I wonder who picked it out*, Clara thought, given Marsha's lack of family.

Sun glinted off more roses repeated in the pattern of the brushed-nickel decorative corners. Someone cared very deeply for the dearly departed and in a romantic way. She started scanning bereaved faces to see if she could figure out who when Mag swore and the sound of a walker thumped closer and closer from behind.

Hagatha wore a pair of rubber rain boots in a garish plaid pattern, which wouldn't have been so noticeable if she hadn't paired them with a matching tam-o'-shanter hat, the pom-pom on top bobbing with every step. At least she was fully dressed, even if she did look like a toddler searching for a good mud puddle to stomp through.

No sooner had that thought crossed Clara's mind when the scent of magic tickled her nose and the sound of bagpipes rent the air. If there'd been any question about the source of the plaintive music, Hagatha's saucy wink and grin put all doubt to rest.

"Feels like herding ducks on a treadmill," Mag snarled.

"You deal with her. I'll handle the cleanup." Clara spotted several coven members clustered around Penelope, the lot of them doing their level best to avoid locking eyes with her. Anything to keep from being dragged into one of Hagatha's little dramas. Fine. Let them cower like chickens.

Pulling from the center of her power and letting it flow up and out like water, Clara crafted an illusion on the fly that, while fuzzy around the edges, would do in a pinch. The piper looked real enough so long as no one got too close. If the other witches didn't like the use of magic in public, they were welcome to handle the problem on their own.

From her outsider's perspective, the Harmony coven, while having a valid reason to worry about being outed by Hagatha, had gone a step too far in the other direction by banning even the smallest spells in public. If they wanted Balefire help to keep their aging high priestess under wraps, they were going to have to lighten up a little. In fact, if they lightened up a little, there might not be the need for anyone to be on Hagatha detail. A circular problem of their own making.

Despite her methods, Hagatha's instinct had been sound—the plaintive tune had left hardly a dry eye in the crowd.

By the time the last strains of "Amazing Grace" wafted into silence, Mag had Hagatha under control. As much as anyone ever did, anyway. It wasn't that they'd intimidated Hagatha into behaving, but that she'd come to pay her respects to the dead, and so she remained subdued until the service ended.

"Hard way to die, but then so's most ways unless you toddle off in your sleep." The old witch commented a little too loudly. "Better than being burned at the stake though, hey?"

"Hush up, you old coot." Mag risked being hexed into the middle of next week, but Hagatha was so caught up she didn't register the hissed command, so the sisters gently ushered her toward the rear of the crowd.

"Drowning. Now there's a good way to go, and if you're lucky, you get to be fish food. Circle of life. Clean, too. That's the best way. Killing's messy. Once you've done the deed, there's always the body to hide. 'Course, sometimes it works out, so murder looks like an accident and that's how the guilty avoid having to pay for their crimes." Hagatha raised her voice to a quavering shout at the end and banged her walker on the ground to make a muffled sound that was part thump and part squelch.

Behind her, Clara heard a startled gasp and the sound of bodies colliding, right before her own breath slammed out of her in a rush as Mag took her down. The sisters hit the ground in a tangle of arms and legs and Mag's cane. Dazed, she gazed up at concerned faces and sighed with relief when someone levered Mag's body off hers. For someone so frail looking, her sister packed a wallop.

"Are you all right?" Leanne Snow's face, tear-stained and blotchy, came into focus.

"Uh, I think so. What happened?"

The man with Leanne, presumably her husband, made sure Mag was solidly on her feet then offered Clara a hand up. He might have started out the day impeccably dressed and smelling good, a scent she recognized, but she'd managed to muddy him up a little as he pulled Clara off the ground. "Human dominoes, and you happened to be on the end of the chain. I'm not sure who started it, though."

That was the question Clara would most like answered since the incident appeared to have been touched off by Hagatha's veiled accusation of murder. Of the handful close enough to have heard Hagatha's challenge, Gertrude Granger and Bryer Mack were the only two people she knew by name. Neither seemed to have a clear-cut motive for killing Marsha, so she directed her search beyond them and saw the back of

Perry Weatherall's head as he cut through the crowd of mourners.

The whole town must have turned out to say their goodbyes. The four rows of chairs facing the coffin were packed, with more people clustered on either side and along the back.

"I'm Dylan Snow, by the way. I think you know my wife." Now that Clara was back on her feet, he cradled Leanne with an arm around her waist, and she leaned heavily against him. "Hell of a way to meet our new neighbors. Sad day for the town, but it's in times like these when you see folks pull together and support each other." His inflection and the way his eyes clouded with pain suggested he'd had a brush with tragedy at some time in the past.

"Yes." Mag injected concern into her voice while she pried gently and rubbed a hand absently over her left hip where it had made contact with Clara's knee. "I only met Marsha once, but I can see she was well-liked. Were the two of you close?"

Both sisters studied his face carefully; It wouldn't be the first time a married man found solace in the arms of another woman.

"She was Leanne's boss and a good friend. Now, if you'll excuse us, Leanne has prepared some remarks for the eulogy, and the service is about to begin." Supporting his wife, Dylan guided her toward the casket where the pastor waited.

Clara quirked an eyebrow at Mag, who gave a slight head shake which Clara answered with a near-imperceptible nod. Unless he was a consummate liar, the knee-jerk reaction to Hagatha's bald assessment of murder had not come from Dylan.

Once the service started, Hagatha fell oddly quiet. Maybe death held more of an allure than life at her age, Clara thought.

Or else she was up to something. With Hagatha, it could go either way.

There were prayers followed by some personal remarks about the deceased, and an introduction to Marsha's cousin from out of town—the only family member to attend the funeral. She appeared to be a few years younger than Marsha had been, and as far as Clara could tell from the back, appeared to be genuinely devastated. Too upset to talk.

When the pastor nodded to Leanne, she stepped forward and spoke eloquently, if tearfully, of her friend. By the time she finished on a choked sob, even Mag had gotten a little misty-eyed.

"I'll miss her forever." With those as her parting words, Leanne broke into something between a fast walk and a trot, right down the center of the aisle between the rows of chairs and kept on going through the cemetery gates, leaving her husband behind. The last anyone saw of her, she was headed back toward town as fast as her high heels would carry her.

One final prayer ended the funeral service, and with nothing left to see, the crowd began to thin out. Hagatha stayed rooted to her spot until everyone else had gone except for Mag, Clara, and the undertaker who triggered the mechanism that lowered the casket into the ground.

"It's time to go now." Clara gently tried to pull the elderly witch away.

"You can go. I'm going to stay right here. I want to see this."

"What do you think is going to happen?"

Dead witches departed this world amid the flames of a funeral pyre, either built on land or on a small barge, to be set adrift so the smoke could carry them to the Summerlands. To Clara's way of thinking, the practice of burying the dead and putting up monuments was sheer hubris.

75

To Hagatha, the process was fraught with high drama, a spectacle to watch with avid curiosity. Or maybe she hoped to catch a glimpse of the grim reaper. After all, she'd escaped his clutches for years untold. Whatever her reason, the Balefire sisters finally left her to it. Cleaning up her magical messes might fall under their current list of responsibilities, but her day-to-day care and feeding was someone else's problem.

"We're done here, right?" Without waiting for the answer, Mag made for the cemetery exit closest to the ice cream stand. "I wore the clothes, I went to the thing, I nearly broke a hip, and now it's butter-pecan time."

"You're welcome for the soft landing," Clara said, brushing the dirt off her clothes. "I've got skid marks on my ribs that'll be there for a week, there's mud seeping into my backside, and we're no closer to knowing who killed Marsha than we were before. Ice cream won't cure any of that."

"Make me less cranky, though."

"Well, I suppose that's one benefit." Locking her arm through Mag's, Clara checked for anyone nearby, then chanced a drying spell on her clothes and matched her sister's pace.

From the outside, the town looked like it always had: a little sleepy, a place where neighbors helped each other, and children played without fear. Mag had called it about the seedy underbelly, though. The person who killed Marsha was someone she had known. Someone she probably trusted, and that was the saddest part. Moreover, the killer was getting away with murder.

Caught up in her thoughts, Clara didn't answer the first time Mag spoke, and it wasn't until she felt a jab in her already sore ribs that she came back to the present.

"What? That hurt. Are you trying to make a permanent dent?"

"Wimp. Look." Mag pointed to an unexpected sight. Leanne Snow, still in her funeral attire, pulling a metal dolly-type cart down the sidewalk. It was a flatbed with a tall handle, like the ones at the big chain building-supply stores, and was piled with heavy-looking boxes.

"Are you thinking what I'm thinking?"

"That Leanne had the means to move the body as well as the opportunity? Yes, and maybe that husband of hers wasn't as attentive as he seemed. She was right there when Hagatha made that murder comment. Looks like Leanne's back on the list."

Chapter Eight

"Need some help with that?" Clara's voice nearly startled Leanne out of her skin as she maneuvered the overloaded cart up her front walkway.

Arms too tanned for the current season and the ever-present layer of foundation that looked troweled on evidenced Leanne's attempts to slow the ravages of time. Clara could have prescribed an essential oil blend that would have done the trick with far less effort and a more natural-looking result.

Sculpted biceps flexed with the effort, and Clara wondered why Leanne felt she had to try so hard, and whether enough gym time to cultivate that level of strength had been for looks or for another, more deadly reason.

"I've got it; don't trouble yourself," Leanne's surprise smoothed into a welcoming smile too light to completely cover the signs of grief. Maybe she was one of those people who found solace in physical labor.

When Mag toddled up behind her sister, Leanne took one look and resigned herself to the fact that she'd have to invite the Balefires inside. Only Clara recognized the sheen of sweat on Mag's face for a carefully-constructed glamour spell. "Would you like a glass of lemonade? You look positively dreadful."

Mag swallowed the urge to reply with the vim and vigor that bubbled into her throat like bile and instead made the unusual decision to play nice. For the moment, at least. "Yes, please, that would be lovely."

"We don't have much time before her husband gets back, I'd wager. Let's make this quick." Clara whispered when Leanne had deposited them in her floral-themed living room and retreated to the kitchen for refreshments.

"So, what you're saying is, we need to pull the truth out of her?" Mag flashed Clara a mischievous grin as Leanne returned with a pitcher and some glasses, and took a shot in the dark. "So, Leanne, tell us why you lied about hurrying home to put the kids to bed on the night Marsha died."

"Excuse me?" Leanne sputtered, her gaze traveling from Mag to Clara, who she apparently judged as the saner of the pair. "What is your mother talking about?"

Clara glared at Mag who returned the look with a little wink. "I'm just going to cut to the chase. We think—no, we're sure Marsha didn't fall from that bridge by accident. And equally certain she didn't jump on purpose, though that seems to be the consensus around town." She paused to let the implications set in.

"You're not being honest about something, so unless you want us to go have a little chat with the police, I'd suggest you fess up." Clara's tone was the embodiment of sweetness and light, exactly like a grandmother's—when she's had enough and is getting ready to lower the boom.

"First of all, like I told you before, Marsha was my friend, and I would never do anything to hurt her. And no, I didn't go straight home that night. You want to know my big secret? See what it is I'm hiding? Hold on." Leanne stomped down the hallway, the sounds of her rummaging around in the next room covered by a hurried conversation.

"What do you think you're doing? We didn't agree to accuse her of anything."

"You wanted the truth, didn't you? I figured she was lying about something. Everyone does."

"I hope she's not looking for a gun." Clara cast Mag a steely-eyed glare and readied a shield spell in case it was needed.

Leanne returned with a large white envelope, threw it on the coffee table, and stood back expectantly, her hands on her hips.

Clara shrugged and pulled out a sheaf of photo proofs, her eyes widening and her cheeks flushing crimson with the effort not to grin. "She has an alibi."

Mag snatched the photos from Clara's hands and let out a low whistle, "How do these prove anything, except that women these days have zero decorum?"

"There's a time stamp, *Mother*. And something tells me these are for Leanne's husband's eyes only." Clara certainly hoped Leanne wasn't planning on handing out photos of herself, spread-eagle and wearing nothing but a few strategically-placed wisps of a feather boa.

"Yes, of course, they are. And for me a little, too. A post-baby-weight pick-me-up to bolster my confidence. Was I supposed to get your permission first?" The admission came with the kind of difficulty that often stemmed from a history of self-esteem issues. *If only the woman could see her own beauty*. Clara thought a clear vision spell wouldn't go amiss and nearly gave in to the temptation.

"I—*we're*—sorry for...well, everything. But the fact remains that *someone* killed your friend. Maybe you can help us find out who."

Leanne's ire gave way to fresh grief as she considered the implications of Clara's statement, "Yes, maybe. I'll do whatever I can. But why aren't the police investigating, if it was murder?"

"We don't have any hard evidence and Cobb certainly isn't going to go out of his way to look deeper into what he assumes is a cut-and-dried accident."

"So when you threatened me before, that was—"

"Call it motivation."

Leanne raised an eyebrow, "Well played."

"Tell us what you know about Marsha. Did she have enemies? Was she involved with anyone? That kind of thing."

Leanne took a seat on an overstuffed chair across from Mag and Clara and heaved an enormous sigh. "I've heard the rumors, and most of them are ridiculous, not to mention way off base. Marsha wasn't private because she was hiding some deep, dark secret—and if I'm wrong, I didn't know my friend nearly as well as I thought I did. She was private because of what happened before she moved back to town."

Falling silent, Leanne bit her lip. Betraying Marsha's confidence might be necessary, but it wouldn't come easy.

"It's okay, you're not betraying her; you're helping her, even if it does feel like a breach of confidence. I know we're strangers, and that we came on a little strong, but please believe we only want to find justice for Marsha." Clara considered using magic to show Leanne their true intentions but instead gave the woman a few moments to come to terms with her statement. After what felt like an eternity, Leanne nodded, swallowed hard, and continued.

"Marsha had a turbulent—and somewhat inappropriate— relationship with a high-profile journalist who just happened to be her superior at the time. When a rival reporter found out about the affair—and it was an affair, though Marsha thought he and his wife were estranged—she leaked the story to another news outlet and effectively ended Marsha's career." She slid the pictures back into the envelope.

"This all happened right around the time Marsha's grandfather died and left her the Harmony Holler," she continued. "She came home, settled down, and kept her personal past private. Of course, there are enough busybodies in this town to fill a turnip truck, and they're not all technologically handicapped."

She sighed. "I wouldn't call it public knowledge, but I'm almost positive there are a few people who were aware of Marsha's indiscretion. Still, that business was put to bed years ago, and I can't see how it could have anything to do with her death."

"Unless," Mag spoke up for the first time, "the rumors about another clandestine affair are true, and Marsha had been seeing someone else in town. Someone who wasn't exactly available."

If Leanne thought her husband had been embroiled in a dalliance with Marsha, her face would give it away, Mag was certain, and her eyes narrowed as she watched for the telltale reaction.

Leanne shifted uncomfortably in her seat and busied herself with picking an imaginary piece of lint from the arm of the chair. "If Marsha had a lover, she didn't see fit to confide in me, but I've suspected there was someone special lately. She never was a fashionista, but over the last few months, she'd upgraded her wardrobe to include higher hemlines and lower necklines. I noticed she'd added more frequent salon appointments to her calendar, and started a gym membership. She seemed happy, for the first time in a long time."

"So, it's possible she *was* seeing someone she shouldn't have been?"

"No. I don't believe Marsha would make that mistake again."

"But you can't know for sure." Mag prodded without remorse.

Clara shot her a look that could cut glass and rolled her eyes, "What makes you so certain, Leanne?"

"Well, about six years ago, when Mary Mountain and Johnny Farber got married, we rode the limo bus into Port Harbor for an over-the-top bachelorette party. I'm no prude, and neither was Marsha, but a male strip club really wasn't either of our scenes, so we stayed behind and cleaned out most of the champagne from the mini bar. It was the first time she ever let her guard down with me, and that's the night our friendship began." Leanne's eyes misted over at the memory.

"Anyway, she broke down and told me the whole story. How she'd been duped into believing everything her boss had said about the rocky relationship between him and his wife. For crying out loud, she was in her early twenties at the time, and to hear her tell it, he had charisma coming out his ass. She wasn't the first, and I doubt she was the last. She told me how she'd followed him home one night only to watch him playing a convincing Ward Cleaver to his wife and kids. It crushed her, and she broke off the relationship. Marsha said she'd never be put in that position again, and that it was the biggest regret of her life."

"Why keep this new man a secret then?"

"I assumed she was exercising caution, keeping her private life private. I refuse to believe otherwise. This had to be about something else, but I can't imagine what."

"What about the argument over the lease agreement with Perry Weatherall? Some people are insinuating the two of them were sworn enemies, and he didn't corroborate your story about being at the office on the night of Marsha's death."

Leanne's mouth gaped open in surprise, "He most certainly was there; he walked in just as I was leaving for my appointment with the photographer."

83

"He seemed to think you might be mistaken—that you might not have been wearing your glasses," Clara hedged.

"Well, I don't see what that has to do with anything! They pinch behind my ears and make red marks across my nose. I can see just fine without them." Leanne's tone was defensive, but her pink-tinged cheeks told another story. "I distinctly remember coming out the door and twisting my ankle on the stoop. I thought I was going to land on my face, but someone caught me. He reeked of Paco Rabanne, which I detest, and it's part of why I tend to stay as far away from Perry Weatherall as humanly possible."

"I apologized for slamming him in the shins with my purse and asked him to replace the blown lightbulb, and he replied, 'No problem,' and handed the purse back to me."

"You're absolutely positive it was Perry?"

"I'm sure." A measure of uncertainty undetectable by any human not trained in the art of lie detecting, but plain as day to witches of Balefire caliber crept into Leanne's voice. "It had to be him."

"What can you tell us about the controversy surrounding the paper's lease agreement?"

"That? Old news." Before Leanne had time to elaborate, the front door swung open and a three- or four-year-old with flying pigtails, a sunny smile, and her daddy's eyes raced toward her mother. An older woman pushing a stroller that looked like it might have been born in a back room at NASA followed her.

"I'm sorry, dear. I didn't realize you had company. The baby just fell asleep." The newcomer introduced herself as Leanne's mother-in-law. "I'll just go put him down for you, shall I?"

Without learning anything else of value, Mag and Clara said their goodbyes.

A few minutes later, over the long-delayed cone of ice cream, Mag commented, "Doesn't it strike you as odd the dead woman kept her life so private even her closest friends didn't know who she was dating, yet half the town showed up for her funeral?"

Clara wagged her finger at her sister. "Don't you get started on one of your wild conspiracy theories, Margaret Balefire. This is a small town, and Marsha's job put her in contact with many from the community. That's all there is to it."

"Think what you like, but someone had a motive for killing Marsha, and we're no closer to finding it than we were before. Unless..." Pivoting and thumping her cane on the ground, Mag muttered and stomped the three blocks back to Leanne's house without telling Clara why.

When Leanne opened the door, Mag asked one question, "Did you notice anything missing when you got to the office on the day after Marsha died?"

"You mean like money? We never kept a lot of cash on the premises. Everyone pays with plastic these days."

"And everything looked just the same as you left it the night before?" Mag prodded. "Think hard, it's important."

Leanne closed her eyes to bring back the mental image of the time before the Balefire sisters had broken the sad news.

"There was something, now I'm thinking about it. But I didn't think anything of it at the time."

Practically dancing in place, Mag prodded, "What was missing?"

"The photographs of the clock tower. The digitally enhanced set. I just figured Marsha took them home with her as a keepsake. She was so excited about how much extra detail they were able to pull from the negatives." A fresh mist of tears sheened Leanne's eyes. "I assumed she wanted them as a memento once we'd sent everything to the printers."

"So the paper will come out as usual?"

"Yes. A fitting tribute to her last day."

Clara needed no scrying crystal to see the gears turning in Mag's head since she'd come to a similar conclusion, and that was why, halfway home, the sisters faced each other and spoke at once.

"We have to get into Marsha's house."

"Fancy a little breaking and entering?"

Chapter Nine

"What are you wearing? Combat boots?" The sound of Clara's soles hitting the stairs grated on Mag's nerves. "Have I taught you nothing?"

"Don't get your panties in a twist, I made silencing charms for each of us." Mag accepted the pull tab from a can of soda when Clara handed it back over her shoulder.

"Recycling again?" Wild unicorns couldn't drag the admission out of Mag, but she envied Clara's ability to enchant everyday objects. As talents went, it was a real time saver not to have to craft charms from metal, clay, wood, or stone before imbuing them with magic.

"Waste not, want not. Rub your thumb over it three times to activate and give it two firm squeezes to end the spell."

"Single-use?"

"Cleanse in running water after every third go and this baby will last forever. One of my better charms, don't you think?"

"Mmph." Most days, Margaret would insist she had made peace with losing the best and last part of her youthful beauty to an unexpected encounter with a Raythe. A simple charm like the one she now held in her hand, a charm made with barely a whisper of effort, would have hidden her approach, given her the edge.

As fresh now as though the fifty years between that moment and this had never passed, Mag replayed the scene in her head. The raging desperation, the blood-pounding rush of fear when the Raythe's power snaked around her neck, and she knew she would die alone on the windy crag.

Ginger hair had curtained her face as she was yanked from her feet into thin air. Vanity. Pure vanity had kept her from shearing the length when shorter would have been more convenient. Vanity kept the Raythe's gaze from connecting fully with hers, and vanity had saved her.

It had been a close thing, though, as she felt her soul, the very essence of her magic, being siphoned. Sucked from her like water through a straw. And when an errant breeze whipped the curling mass into a proper shield, she saw it turn white even as the magic leaped inside her again.

Maybe her faerie Godmother had been watching—Mag would never know—but she took what power welled up, molded it into a weapon, and burned that Raythe to ash, vowing never to count the cost.

A vow she mostly kept.

"It's broad daylight. Won't it be weird if people can see us but not hear us coming?"

"Your enthusiasm is underwhelming." In a fit of pique, Clara stomped across the porch without looking back, raised the hand holding the charm, and rubbed it with an exaggerated motion. Mag trudged through the icy silence left behind in Clara's wake.

Figuring there was a fifty-fifty chance anything she said would make it worse, Mag stayed quiet and let Clara march off the rare huff that was something of a role reversal between them.

Clara had wanted to wait for nightfall to go on this fishing expedition, but Mag insisted daylight was better, easier to hide their presence without having to turn on lights. It was the last house on the street and hidden from view of its neighbors by a curve in the road. Approaching from the river walk rather than the road would be enough for them to remain unseen.

"Feels like there ought to be crime scene tape over the door," Mag said. Not that it would have caused so much as a twitch on either sister's moral compass; they had right on their side. The lock surely didn't slow them down. Drawing on the well of power burning in her core, she let the magic flow into the keyhole like smoke. A muted click sounded, and the door inched open.

"We're the only ones who know there even *was* a crime," Clara reminded her. "Well, besides Marsha's killer, anyway. Any idea what we're looking for?"

Mag thought for a moment. "The missing images, and failing that, something that speaks to motive. Once we have the why, it shouldn't be hard to find the who."

Justice drove Mag as it always had, the thrill of the hunt jittering in her gut, pushing the blood through her veins, and setting her senses tingling. Marsha might rest in peace while her killer walked free, but Mag would not.

"And then what?" Clara asked.

"He pays. Most crimes are committed for one of three reasons: love, money, or revenge. A woman in her position, it could be any one of them. We'll start with the love angle since it doesn't look like Marsha was rolling in the dough." Mag cast a trained eye over the furniture, the contents of the shelves. Good pieces, she noted, serviceable but nothing valuable. And nothing seemed out of place.

Marsha kept a ruthlessly organized office at work, but her home showed another side of the newspaper editor. Sunlight streamed through a collection of colored bottles lined up on the sills of six clerestory windows to create colored splashes on the polished oak floor.

Built-in shelves spanned from floor to ceiling in the rest of the living space. Mag recognized the telltale signs of a would-be do-it-yourselfer: a few jagged edges and a couple of crooked angles only added to the lived-in, homey vibe she felt sure Marsha had purposely cultivated. Rows and stacks of books on topics ranging from the political climate of Saudi Arabia to the life and times of Abraham Lincoln were punctuated by tomes dedicated to the cultivation of various herbs and a number of field guides for the seasoned hiker.

Marsha Hutchins had been a strong, well-rounded woman if Mag's instincts were correct—and if she knew one thing to be true, it was that strong, well-rounded women usually had a few skeletons in their closet.

The one adjacent to Marsha's living room merely contained boxes of volumes not deemed worthy of shelf space. When Mag dusted off the cover of a trashy romance novel, her estimation of the dead woman rose a couple notches higher. *We've all got our guilty pleasures*, she thought, smiling a little while rummaging through the rest of the coat closet and coming up with nothing more than a niggling wish to have gotten to know the editor a little better before her life was snuffed out—and even more motivation to find her murderer.

Letting her eyes drop closed, Mag cast her senses out in a widening circle. Her power crept over oak floors that begged for the touch of a sander and new coat of stain but came up with nothing sinister. What had she hoped to find, anyway? A flashing neon sign with the killer's name on it?

While Mag searched the kitchen, Clara made her way through the bedroom to the adjoining bath. If Marsha had a lover who came around on more than a casual basis, there should be some evidence—a razor, a toothbrush, something. A thorough search of the medicine cabinet and the stuffed-to-capacity drawers beneath the wash basin provided little information save for the fact that Marsha enjoyed the buy-four-get-one-free sales at Bath and Body Works, and preferred the smell of cucumber-melon above all others.

Something drew her attention to a nearly hidden linen cabinet tucked behind the bathroom door. Whether it was a gentle waft of a more masculine, huskier scent or simply her Balefire instincts, Clara didn't stop to wonder. She rarely questioned the hows and whys of being a witch, preferring to accept the gifts she'd been given without requiring a scientific qualification to explain them.

If she'd been put on the spot regarding the topic, Clara would cite faith as one of her guiding principles, knowing without a doubt that her sister would stand on the opposite side of the fence. For Mag, magic was a puzzle to be solved—for Clara, it just *was*, and she was okay not having all the answers.

Inside the cabinet—along with enough tubes of toothpaste to make Clara wonder if Marsha was preparing for a zombie apocalypse—sat a navy blue, woven basket that she recognized as the one thing unlike all the others. Shades of white and a soft, buttery yellow had been Marsha's preference; this item was chosen for someone else—someone with more masculine tastes.

"Maggie, I found something." Clara beckoned her sister into the bedroom, then dumped the contents onto Marsha's bed.

"Well, she was definitely seeing someone, and it wasn't just a fling. Men don't tend to keep Rogaine at their girlfriend's house unless they're fairly comfortable," Mag snickered.

"And these are high-end shaving supplies—whoever he is, he's got expensive taste." Clara picked up an electric beard

91

trimmer and pulled a few coarse hairs from the blade with the resigned look of a mother who's gotten used to sticking her hands in all manner of disgusting substances. "And he's got brown hair. Well, so do half the men on the planet. That's not particularly helpful."

"Biology 101, Clarie. It's a DNA sample—witch-style. All we need is a match. Here, collect as much as you can." Mag whipped a corked glass bottle from the leather tool belt she habitually wore beneath the fashion debacle of the day and handed it to her sister.

"Have fun with that. I'm definitely not It, if *It* involves plucking the hairs of strange men all over town."

Mag didn't dignify that with a retort, opting instead to rifle through the nightstand drawers. Finding nothing more illuminating, the pair exited to the hallway, where a secretary desk positioned against the opposite wall caught their attention.

Clara took two long strides, flung open the roll top, and began rummaging through the cubbies and compartments.

"It's mostly bills and receipts," she said. "I sincerely hope Marsha didn't keep her business records as disorganized as her personal ones, or whoever takes over as editor is going to have their work cut out for them."

Mag yanked on each of the lower drawers in turn before sighing and uttering a spell under her breath. At her command, the foot-thick pile of papers straightened itself into a neat ream and began self-sorting into piles. Anything deemed inconsequential went back into the drawers, leaving a modest stack for Mag and Clara to sift through.

"No personal correspondence of any kind, though that doesn't surprise me in this day and age. She probably did everything on her *smart*phone. Such an oxymoron, I mean really—" Mag's mumbling abruptly silenced and a second later she waved a few sheets of paper in Clara's face, "Look at this. Talk about a smoking gun."

Clara studied the documents and let out a low whistle, "Perry Weatherall is in a deep financial hole, and Marsha has the evidence. Looks like he's liquidating his assets in a hurry."

"And taking some pretty steep losses."

"How can you tell?" Between the pair of them, Clara thought herself the more financially savvy. Mag could haggle a deal with the best of them, but when it came down to spreadsheets and charts, she let her sister do the heavy lifting.

"I can do math, can't I? And didn't we just purchase property here? You and that real estate agent droned on for hours about this stuff." She pointed to one of the entries. "Three-thousand square feet on Dewberry lane and he let it go for seventy-five percent of market value. Condition looks good, too. In today's market, he could have upped the price by another ten grand and still caught the easy sale. It's like he's giving properties away."

"Well, I didn't think you were listening." In retrospect, Clara realized she should have known. Mag rarely missed anything.

"This is a lot of ammunition, Mag said, flipping through them again, paying closer attention to details. "Enough to expose Perry as a financial adviser who didn't take his own advice. Do you think she was going to print something in the paper?"

"Looks like Perry had an excellent motive for murder after all."

A wave of Mag's hand sent the desk back into its former state of disarray.

"Nobody here to see, so I'm taking the quick route home," Mag gathered herself together and prepared to shift and skim through space.

Clara checked her watch to see what the hurry was all about. "You just want to spy on the mailman."

"Maybe. I've got a box of vintage linens that should have been here yesterday. Pyewacket found them on the computer. A place called Itty Bitty. No, that's not it. Eensy? I can't remember."

"You mean Etsy?"

"That's it."

"You know I could teach you to use the…" Before Clara could say computer, Mag was gone. "Never mind." She said to the empty house and let herself out into the fine, warm mist that had begun to fall—the kind that sometimes falls on an otherwise sunny day and dries almost before it hits the ground. The kind that always made Clara's feet want to dance.

Her face turned up to catch the soft wash on her skin, little beads of moisture clinging and shining like diamonds in her hair, and she smiled in pure joy. Norm McCreery gazed at her in awe, as if she looked like a fairytale princess, when he ran into her on his way back to the town hall.

"Clara." He nodded and couldn't help it when his gaze drifted down to take in the whole of her.

"Mayor McCreery." She nodded back and hoped he wouldn't stop to chat.

"A word if you don't mind." And there went hope, dashed to bits.

She dipped her head. "Of course. What can I do for you?"

The mayor fell into step beside her, shortening his stride to match hers and cementing her opinion of him as a gentleman.

"I wanted to check in with you and make sure you're all right. Finding that body must have been quite a shock to you and your mother."

Clara appreciated the gesture of concern, unnecessary though it was. "Death is always a shock, isn't it? Even though it's coming for all of us, eventually. Honestly, I'm glad we happened across poor Marsha when we did. Goddess knows how long she might have lain there, and I'd have hated for someone else to find her—like one of the children who play in those woods."

Norm McCreery cocked an eyebrow at Clara's reference to the goddess, but didn't comment.

"Ah, so you're an optimist then?" His sidelong smile bordered on flirtatious, and Clara quickly changed the subject.

"How's that oatmeal cream working out for you?" She asked, hoping the mention of his erratic behavior at Marsha's funeral would dampen his spirits.

Instead, it only seemed to bolster his spirits when, with a grin and a wink he retorted, "Like magic."

Without a suitable reply, Clara made an excuse to exit the conversation, and with a sigh of relief, parted ways and headed in the direction of home.

She had just rounded the last bend in the road when the slap of tennis shoes on pavement drew close behind her. Clara silently cursed the gods, wondering what the good mayor wanted now. Instead of the rosy-cheeked Norm McCreery, she came face-to-face with a jogging-pants-clad Bryer Mack.

"Oh, hello there." He stopped just short of running her over, executing a last-minute hop-skip combination that nearly landed him in a prickly bush.

"Hello, Bryer. Beautiful day for a jog." Clara indicated the azure blue sky.

Bryer looked up at the cloudless dome as if seeing it for the first time. "Sure is, I thought I'd take advantage of it, but I'm having an off day. Usually, I take the footpath by the bridge and run through the woods. Of course, since Marsha…well, I thought a new route might be in order."

"Understandable," Clara said, sighing. "I'm not sure I'll ever be able to walk that path again without seeing her there. So tragic. On a good note, Leanne says they've managed to pull the paper together, so at least Marsha's final project will see the light of day. I imagine she'd be happy about that, though of course, I barely knew the woman."

Bryer's eyebrows shot up toward his hairline. "They're still releasing the paper?"

She nodded. "Sounds like. I guess they'd finished the layout and sent it to the printers just before, you know…it happened. Leanne's determined to honor Marsha's memory by putting out the final paper even if she's doing it without pay. Poor girl, everyone thinks she's a ditz, but I rather like her."

"Leanne is a character, but she's loyal. And you're right, she's sharper than anyone gives her credit for." Jogging in place to keep his heart rate up, Bryer seemed impatient to get on with his exercise, so Clara wished him well and sent him on his way.

Chapter Ten

"Get out the phone book, Clarie, and find out where Perry lives. It's about time we had a private conversation, don't you think?"

Clara grinned and held her cell phone aloft. "Nobody uses phone books anymore, Maggie, unless they're missing a sofa leg or something. See, so much faster." She tapped on the screen and read aloud, "Weatherall, Perry and Linda. 102 Church Street. Bingo."

"Well, that's handy, I suppose," Mag admitted begrudgingly.

Clara withheld the *I told you* so bubbling into her throat and instead summoned Pyewacket, who entered from the backyard with Jinx on her tail. A few stray leaves in her hair when she morphed out of cat form proved the two of them had been enjoying some proximity to nature, and Clara doubted there was a live field mouse within a three-mile radius.

"Mind the store for us while we're gone, please. We shouldn't be long."

"And keep Hagatha away from the greenhouse, or else," Mag said, narrowing her eyes.

"We know, we know—kitty kibble for a month." Jinx finished with an uncharacteristic eye roll.

Mag followed Clara down the cobbled path, through the backyard, and onto the trail leading into town. Church Street, which as its name suggested, was home to not one but two different houses of worship: the ambivalently-named Church of God, and a Unitarian Universalist congregation that touted acceptance of all religions.

Mag wasn't exactly sure how that worked out in practice, but they did celebrate the solstices and pronounced *Samhain* correctly, so she figured they were on the right track when it came to modernized Paganism. She'd have suspected old Haggie had something to do with it, but slowly introducing the beliefs of witchkind into popular culture was too subtle for the Hagatha she knew.

Why use a candle when you could light the whole sky with a fireworks show worthy of the Fourth of July?

The winding path through the woods would deposit them near the front of the clock tower. From there it was a hop, skip, and jump through the cemetery, where the eastern exit opened onto Church Street. Faster than walking through town, but their chosen route was rife with déjà vu. Mag couldn't tamp down the image burned into her brain of the expression on Marsha's face when Chief Cobb had pulled her out into the light.

"Creepy, huh?"

"No matter how many times I come face to face with what one person can do to another, it's always unsettling." Mag shook her head sadly.

By the time they'd reached the far end of the graveyard and spilled out onto a provincial, white-birch-lined street, sunset pinked the sky. Mag and Clara had managed to shake off most of the lingering heebie-jeebies and were raring to confront their prime suspect.

"102. It's that Victorian with the wrap-around porch." Clara pointed, her steps quickening, and left Mag tottering two paces behind. She jabbed the bell, and the door opened with a whoosh just as Mag caught up.

"Hello. Can I help you?" A woman in her early forties— not their intended interrogation subject at all—answered the door. She had a nondescript yet pleasant face that lacked the symmetry to be considered pretty. Had she been a character in an eighteenth-century novel, the assumed Mrs. Weatherall would have been described as handsome.

"We're looking for your husband, Perry. I'm Margaret, and this is my daughter, Clara. Town celebration business. Is he home?"

"I'm Linda. You must be our newest additions," she smirked, "because everyone around here knows he hasn't lived here since last summer. I suggest you check his apartment; it's right above the Harmony Holler office." Linda bade Mag and Clara a bitter 'good day' and clicked the door shut in their faces.

"Well, isn't that convenient?" Mag crowed while the pair made their way back down Church Street and into town. "We've already established that Perry had a motive, and he's strong enough to have done the damage and dumped the body, so he had the means."

Clara's mind had taken another track when she heard the news that Perry and his wife were estranged, and she wanted to think through the possible implications.

"And he lives right upstairs, so there's the opportunity," Mag finished, not noticing her sister's preoccupation. "Lends more weight if Leanne was correct, and the man she bumped into that night was Perry after all. Now, we just have to crack his alibi. Or crack him; whichever comes first."

In spring, dusk fell early, so in the glowing light from the second-story window, a flickering, shadowy outline indicated that someone was moving around in Perry's apartment. Just as Clara reached out to press the intercom system's doorbell button, a gray and white tabby cat pounced onto the open window ledge and stared down at her through slitted eyes.

When the bell pealed, he jumped a full foot in the air, spun around, and took off into the apartment. A loud crash, followed by a bang and an ungentlemanly expletive preceded the buzz that unlatched the downstairs door so Mag and Clara could enter.

When Perry appeared at the door, his normally impeccable hair looked mussed, and he limped a little on his left foot. For the first time, Clara took a good, long look at the man's face. She'd studied him while Mag had asked probing questions in the square a few days prior, but this time her gaze held a level of scrutiny her sister would admire.

If the man was a killer, he hid it well. Even annoyed as he was by whatever calamity the cat had caused, he seemed affable enough. And he was a cat person. Even if people don't recognize evil, cats do.

They also recognize witches. Or this one did, anyway. He pranced right up to Mag and tried to climb her like a tree.

"Stop that, Max. It's not polite. I'm sorry, he's not usually like this."

"Max is it?" Mag reached down to give the tabby a scratch behind the ears. "He's a handsome one, isn't he?"

How can I help you, ladies?" The questioning look on his face spoke volumes: clearly, they were the last people he'd expected to find ringing his bell. The undertone of uncertainty in his voice probably had something to do with the nature of the interrogation he'd received last time he'd talked to them.

All of a sudden, Clara wondered whether approaching him privately, so close to the place where they suspected he'd already committed murder, had been the best idea. Of course, she and Mag could protect themselves, but depending on how much they might need to use, resorting to magic could blow the top off the secret they'd been sent to Harmony to keep under wraps in the first place.

It was too late to do anything about it now, and any excuse other than the truth for their unexpected visit would fall flat. Clara thought about Marsha, and how her life had been cut far too short, then resigned herself to whatever outcome the universe had in store.

"You can answer a couple questions for us. About Marsha Hutchins." Perry turned away, leading them to a pair of sofas near the front windows to hide the pained expression that flitted across his face.

"This again? You two are awfully concerned about someone you didn't even know. Why are you poking your noses in where they don't belong?" He asked, his hands clenching into fists at his sides.

"Because we know Marsha was murdered, and so do you." It wasn't an outright accusation, but Mag let a hint of power echo through her voice. Magic danced along her arms, lifted the tiny hairs into quivering attention and slid toward Perry like mist.

He gestured toward one of the sofas, waited for Mag and Clara to settle in.

His defiant expression deflated like a week-old balloon as he sank into an armchair and held his head in his hands. "The truth is, Marsha and I were dating. No, it was more than that. We were in love, and I would never have hurt her. But, you're right; I think someone else did. She was supposed to meet me at Derby's Pub out on Route 15—that dive bar with all the pool tables—after she put the paper to bed that night. It was our six month anniversary and, for a dive bar, the food's good."

Over the next half hour, Perry talked about how his marriage had ended, not with a bang, but a whimper. The assets he'd been selling had gone to pay alimony, and he'd become involved with Marsha only after trying to evict her in order to sell the building that housed the newspaper office.

"She fought back. Tracked me to Derby's where I was drowning my sorrows in cheap whiskey, and pinned back my ears. Asked why I was such a miserable excuse for a human and told me she'd haul my ass to court if I didn't back down."

He swallowed hard a couple of times, then continued. "Next thing I know, I'm pouring out my heart to her, and she's slugging down my drink and one-upping me with her own tale of heartbreak: an affair that derailed her career. We got drunk and ended up at her place for what I thought was a one night stand, but it turned into more."

"You kept it quiet, though? Even after she died? You must have told someone."

"It was what she wanted. Marsha was a private woman, and she wasn't ready to go public with our relationship, so I respected her wishes. It was the last thing I could do for her."

"When was the last time you heard from her?" Clara asked gently.

"She left me a voicemail." Pulling out his phone, he dialed his mailbox, tapped the speaker button, and let them listen.

"Hey babe, we hit a snag, and I'm going to be late. I'll be there as soon as I can. Happy anniversary." Marsha sounded distracted.

"I waited until eight or so, ordered a couple burgers to go, and when she didn't show, I figured she was still tied up at work. The office was dark when I finally made it back here. I took a spin past her place, which was also dark, and her car was parked out front. That was around 9 o'clock."

"That didn't strike you as odd or unusual?"

102

"It might have, but we'd had a minor disagreement over that stupid printer and her refusal to use it for the special edition. I figured she was still annoyed with me, and the stress might have triggered one of her migraines, so she went home to sleep it off. If only I'd been here, I could have saved her life."

Perhaps it was human nature to wish for the ability to change the past, to be able to go back and prevent a wrongdoing—but if it was, the sentiment wasn't exclusive to those without magic. Mag would have given her eye teeth to tweak a few things and rewrite history—for her own sake, as well as Clara's.

"Life is full of shoulda-woulda-couldas, you can't dwell on them, or one day you'll wake up and be wishing you hadn't spent so much time with your best friend, Regret," Mag chided as gently as her gruff nature would allow. "What you can do now is honor her memory, and help us figure out who would have wanted to kill her. Maybe then, she can truly rest in peace."

"How do you *know* Marsha was murdered?" Leanne hadn't asked the one question Clara wasn't sure how to answer, but Perry keyed right in on it, and she wished Mag hadn't been so blunt in opening up the discussion.

"It's more of a suspicion, I suppose. Have you mentioned your concerns to the police?" she deflected.

Perry leaned forward, resting his elbows on his knees. "No evidence. That's the wall I keep hitting, too. It looked like an accident."

"Except for the fact that someone allowed Leanne to think she was speaking to you out on the street that night. It's not enough to spur an official investigation, but it's enough for us. Does anyone else you know use Paco Rabanne? Leanne distinctly identified the fragrance." Clara left out Leanne's unkind comment about Perry's choice of cologne.

"Only half the men in town. The five-and-dime only sells three different scents. It could have been anyone."

They asked a few more questions but gleaned no new information. Perry's confession filled in a few gaps, but provided no new evidence and raised more questions than it answered.

Once back on the street and strolling in the direction of home, Mag said, "It all makes perfect sense now. How could I have been so blind? Don't ever tell me you envy my clairvoyant talents again, Clarie, because they've done absolutely nothing to help us figure out who the real killer is."

She huffed out a breath and shook her head as she shuffled along. "Marsha and Perry might as well have had pink neon hearts flashing above their heads, and all the clues seem so glaringly obvious now, I feel like a fraud."

Mag verbally abused herself for a solid quarter of the trip from town back to their home.

Clara recognized the familiar signs of Mag's impending downward spiral. She felt somewhat defeated too, but there was another part of her heart that smiled knowing Marsha had, in fact, cultivated several healthy relationships during her time on this earth. That was more than a lot of people could say.

"I know it seems dismal now," she said, "but we've eliminated two suspects, and that's an accomplishment— especially considering we don't have a government-sanctioned dossier on the history of every Harmony resident. We started out with a handicap, and we're that much closer to finding the real killer. All we need is a little bit of ingenuity and a dollop of good luck."

Mag considered Clara's statement for a moment, and though it didn't completely lift the doldrums, she felt somewhat heartened as she began mentally sifting through the evidence. "Let's add what Perry told us and run the timeline again. Marsha told Leanne they would be working late. She called Perry and told him the same thing."

Clara picked up where Mag left off. "Leanne left at seven and ran into someone coming into the office as she was leaving. I think we can both agree that it was likely Marsha's killer. If not, that person was the last to see Marsha alive, and if he wasn't the one who murdered her, there would be no reason to lie about it. Especially considering the police aren't even investigating."

Mag scowled when she made the final assessment. "That leaves us with one unanswered question: Who did Leanne run into outside the office? All we know is it was a man, and he wore the same cologne as Perry. Looks like we're back in busybody mode."

"That's fine," Clara said, lifting a shoulder. "When it comes to this I can forget my scruples. What do you think about splitting up tomorrow? You mind the shop, and I'll go into town and get to know our neighbors a little better. If you happen to *accidentally* charm some of our customers into spilling their guts, so be it."

"Whooee, you mean I can finally cut loose with a little magic?"

"I meant with your charming personality, sister mine."

Mag cocked a brow at her. "You do know who you're talking to, right?"

Chapter Eleven

Complain though she might, Margaret Balefire enjoyed every little nuance about selling antiques. Fascinated by the style and craftsmanship of things built to last centuries, she would rather die than step a single toe into IKEA. Spending a morning among the smell of beeswax polish and old furniture, even overlaid by the clean, herbal scents of Clara's concoctions, put a smile on her face.

"You have papers? Provenance?" A customer wearing pink pearls and cashmere demanded.

"You have money? I'll show you mine if you show me yours." Pink pearls meant doodly-squat to Mag when it came to having cash to put in the register. Or that pernicious plastic money everyone used these days.

"I'll give you two hundred."

"That's a Tiffany Studios Nautilus lamp. Mint condition. A steal at three-fifty."

"Throw in the Firestone ashtray, and you've got a deal."

Mag heaved a sigh, but inside she danced as she calculated the profit and rang up the sale. Jinx swathed the lamp in paper and bubble wrap, then carried it to the car. On his way back in, he held the door open for a customer who shoved past like he wasn't even there.

"I need more of this." Practically pocket-sized compared to Jinx's solid form, the woman waved one of the samples Hagatha had charmed. Or cursed depending on how you looked at it. "You have more, right? Can I buy it by the gallon? Or by the case?"

Tossing the sample on the counter, she spotted the display of oatmeal-based products and, jean-clad legs flashing, flung herself in that direction.

"Oh, there's soap, too?" She gathered up three bars and threw them at Jinx who, though stunned, caught them and laid them on the counter beside the register. "And this, and one of these." More products flew across the room—a tube of mask bounced off an urn that probably should have been in a museum, and that was when Mag hit her limit.

"Stop." Enough raw power infused the command that the pixie chick froze on tiptoe, midway through reaching for a cellophane-wrapped bath bomb. A flick of Mag's wrist sent a tingling lash of magic across the room, stripped Hagatha's influence off the woman like peeling the skin off a banana. "That's enough now."

Gentle despite the rising desire to inflict bodily harm on the old witch who was to blame, Mag pulled her energy back.

The woman's face pinked and she looked down. "Maybe just one of the bars of soap. I don't know what I was thinking for a minute there."

"We all get carried away sometimes," Mag said. Jinx and Mag exchanged a look. "The bath bomb is on the house. Unadvertised special, today only."

The minute the door closed behind Hagatha's latest victim, Mag broke into a tirade, but the wail of first one siren, then another, cut it short. The shrill sound raised the hairs on the back of her neck.

"Mind the shop." Curiosity yanked Mag out the door. She stuck her head back in just long enough to issue a second order to Jinx. "And call Clara."

Great gouts of dark smoke cursed the air over the tiny town of Harmony, and Mag wasn't the only person drawn to the source. She fell in with the handful of curious souls headed toward the short block of downtown storefronts.

"It's the newspaper office," several voices chattered.

"Gonna lose the whole block," someone said. "You wait and see. All those buildings are too close together." Others muttered in agreement.

There was a sense of excitement behind the dire predictions—a there-but-for-the-grace way of thinking. Mag ignored all of it and wondered if Clara would find her in the crowd. Being Balefire witches, magic flames fell under the sisters' control so there might be a way they could help. If they wanted to break every coven rule Penelope had penned.

Mag didn't give a flat fig for the rules. Better to save the town than cower like rabbits in the bushes, and any witch worth her ritual salt knew how to work magic in public without being seen. After all, her kind had been hiding in plain sight for practically ever. It was only the random nuts like Hagatha that set out to call attention to themselves and their covens by extension.

Back in Port Harbor, fire engines ran through the city almost every day without causing a mass exodus. Not so in the hamlet of Harmony, where half the town turned up to watch flames dance around the interior of the newspaper office.

Only one person bucked the crowd—Clara caught Mag's eye and hurried over.

"I was headed back to the shop to get you, but I guess you already heard about the fire. Convenient, no?"

"Were you thinking what I'm thinking? Maybe we should..." Mag wiggled her nose and nodded toward the fire. "Looks like the local FD could use a little assistance."

Before Clara had a chance to answer, shouts rang out, and a figure appeared like a specter through the smoke with a body draped over his shoulders in the standard carry position. A flurry of activity near the ambulance blocked their view as the unconscious victim was lowered onto a wheeled stretcher and the med techs took over.

Bryer Mack let the EMT nudge him away from the woman whose life he might have just saved.

"Leanne. It's Leanne Snow. She wasn't supposed to be working today. How could this have happened?" His face looked pale under the streaks of soot as he raised his voice to deliver the grave news. He slumped onto the tailgate of the ambulance and let the attendant strap an oxygen mask over his face, but shook off further assistance.

Lifting the mask off again briefly, he announced, "I'm fine. I'm okay. See to Leanne."

Something brushed against Mag's intuition, a niggling sense that she was needed and right now. Amid such chaos, tuning into the source of the feeling wouldn't be easy, but she knew she had to try. One by one, she shut out the distractions. The hungry crackle of flames as they ate through the building. The tinkle of glass breaking in the heat. The smoke that choked whenever the wind sent it in her direction. The grinding of the pump and rush of water through the hoses, and finally, the shouts of those working to contain the blaze. Above all that, now that she was listening, she heard the plaintive howl of a cat.

"That settles it; we have to do something." Mag practically dragged Clara around the corner of the nearest building where they wouldn't be seen. "Perry's cat is still in the apartment upstairs. We need to save Max."

"And how do you propose we do that without giving anything away? I mean, people are going to notice if we march right up in front and conjure up a storm."

"Listen, I know Hagatha has the coven so cowed they wouldn't risk a spell to stop a sneeze, but this is our town now, and I'm not about to let it burn just because a bunch of weeping weenies can't tell where the line is when it comes to overreacting."

"Fine, but you're in charge of memory charms if this goes bad. I hate messing in people's heads. What did you have in mind? Weather spell? Make it rain? Or we could enchant the fire hoses to pump harder."

The grin that spread across Mag's features pushed back some of the ravages there.

"Balefire." It was her name, her birthright, and a summoning all rolled into one. Balefire flickered between Mag's outstretched hands.

"Ooh, that's genius." Clara picked right up on her sister's intentions. Infecting the raging fire with their namesake would give them the ability not only to walk through the fire unharmed but to put them in control of the hungry flames.

"Not bad if I say so myself. Help me with the sending."

Clara called up her power, laid her hands over Mag's and fed her intention to the ball of flame. Sparks showered them as the fireball sped on the wind of their desire and arrowed toward the newspaper office.

"I'll get the cat, you take care of the rest." With barely a flicker, Mag was gone.

"Sure, take the easy part," Clara said to the empty space where her sister had been. Still, the chance to do magic in a way that counted for something important sent a thrill through her as she rounded the corner and made her way back toward the burning building.

The din of the battle made her pop tab silencing charm useless. An elephant could pass through the crowd on feet rendered silent by the sheer volume of noise, but Clara needed to get close to the newspaper office, so she chose a different charm from her arsenal.

When she rounded the corner, Clara looked exactly like the rest of the firefighters in soot-covered gear, at least to the human eye. Any witch in the crowd would see right past her chameleon charm, but she couldn't be bothered about that as she walked into the inferno, and what looked like certain death.

Flame sprites danced across the floor and slithered up the walls, but from the moment, the magical Balefire had taken over the hungry flames. They ate no more of the newspaper office.

There would be no better time to snoop through the wreckage than right now while the fire held authorities at bay.

"See anything useful?" Mag popped into the room. Angry claws tore their way up her arms, and Max curled around her shoulders, hissing and yowling. "I reckon we have a few minutes to look before we put on the show."

"I don't *see* anything," Clara said, "but the whole place reeks of charcoal starter, and you know what that means."

"It means someone knows we're on the trail and tried to hide evidence. Or worse, kill Leanne Snow. You figure out where it started yet?"

Between the smoke and water damage, there wasn't a lot left to sift through. Both file cabinets had been reduced to twisted, smoldering wrecks, and the desktop computer was a melted ruin. Following her nose, Clara trusted the now-harmless fire to shield her from being visible through the opening that had once held the front window. Bits of safety glass glittered—washed clean by the water still spurting though the building courtesy of the fire department, who had no idea the danger was over.

"The strongest smell is coming from the storeroom. There's probably not much left." Mag followed Clara toward the rear of the office. She was right; piles of ash were all that remained of what she assumed had been boxes of newsprint.

"We'll have to ask Leanne what was in here, but whatever it was, someone wanted it gone."

"If she lives." Grim lines bracketed Mag's mouth, darkened as much by sorrow as soot. "You don't think any of this is our fault, do you? For prying, I mean."

Clara hoped not. Working in tandem, the sisters knocked the fire down by half, set it to subside in a natural-looking way, and heard the firefighters outside shout in triumph. They conjured damp towels from home, wiped off as best they could, and sent the sooty mess back to the laundry room before heading outside to mingle with the crowd.

"Keep a sharp eye out for anyone who smells like fire starter."

"Don't you mean a sharp nose?" Clara's quip, meant to diffuse tension, only netted her a snort from Mag.

In the few minutes it had taken to tame the flames, save the cat—and the town, come to that—whispers of arson were already circulating.

"If there's one thing I hate about small towns, it's the rumor mill," Mag muttered to Clara. "Grinds exceedingly fast, and chews up every grain of truth."

The whispers turned to audible speculation before they were even a block away from the charred remains of the building.

All that paper in an old building? Should have gone up like a torch long before now.

Did you hear? Bryer Mack is a hero. A popular sentiment that spread almost as quickly as the fire had.

Marsha probably set the fire. That theory stopped Clara in her tracks long enough to listen to the cockamamie reasoning behind how Marsha might have accomplished such a feat from beyond the grave. *Some kind of device, set up on a timer to burn evidence and throw off suspicion.*

"Evidence of what?" She couldn't help but ask the snobbish woman who'd said it.

"Er," and a confused look was all she got for an answer. She rolled her eyes and kept walking, keeping an ear out as she went.

You know the building was insured to the hilt. Maybe Perry was trying to scare up funds to pay for his divorce.

Or maybe, Mag thought, *Leanne stumbled on the same piece of information that led to Marsha's murder.* With all evidence either burned or water damaged beyond repair, the only way to find out would be to talk to Leanne herself—if and when she pulled through.

Chapter Twelve

Harmony certainly wasn't big enough to warrant an entire hospital to serve its residents, so Leanne was rushed fifteen miles north to the county facility with what seemed like half the town trailing behind. Mag and Clara hopped into the old VW bus they'd acquired when they decided to leave the city. It didn't have an engine per se, but who needs an engine when you have a world of magic at your disposal?

"So what are your spidey senses telling you, Maggie?" Clara asked when they were almost there. "Because I can see it going one of two ways. Either Leanne was an unintended victim, which means the office itself was targeted; or Leanne hasn't been as forthcoming as she'd like us to believe."

"Or she knows something but doesn't realize its significance. Or, we could be encountering that elusive creature known as a coincidence."

Clara snorted, "Rarer than a polka-dotted unicorn, that one. No, I smell the distinct scent of desperation."

"Me too, and it smells oddly like Paco Rabanne. The trouble is, Perry was right. It's a best seller at the local five and dime. You should start manufacturing some alternatives, Clarie. We could make a fortune."

"I'll get right on that after we catch a killer and foil whatever plot Hagatha's been hatching up when she thinks we're not looking. Slow down, there's the hospital entrance."

As indicated by the cast of characters assembled in the waiting room, it was clear that even though Harmony was home to a powerful coven of witches who made every attempt to fit into "normal" society, there was still a separation between the two groups. Not one coven member had made the short trip, leaving Mag and Clara the only representatives of the magical community in attendance. Not that anyone else noticed.

Leanne's husband, Dylan, managed a grim nod in their direction but spent his time pacing back and forth in front of the formidable double doors marked with a large red stop sign to indicate anyone without an employee badge was unwelcome unless accompanied by someone in scrubs or a white coat.

Several women around Leanne's age were also present, one of whom identified herself as Mary Mountain-Farber, the friend whose wedding Leanne had mentioned previously. Mrs. Green, whose given name was still unknown to the Balefire sisters, cluck-clucked about how she'd been Leanne's babysitter once upon a time, and wasn't it such a terrible tragedy for a fire like that to have occurred in their sleepy little town?

Each well-wisher carried the same expression of concern and anticipation, including Bryer Mack, who arrived last and made a point of aggressively shaking Dylan's hand while uttering the sort of platitudes expected in a dire situation such as this. Dylan, overcome with appreciation for the man who saved his wife's life, wrapped Bryer in a hug. If Bryer's incredulous expression was any indication—was not in keeping with his usual, reserved personality.

"You're welcome," Bryer patted Dylan's back stiffly, "I just did what anyone else would do."

When Dylan was finally ushered into the no trespassing zone amid reassurances that Leanne would make a full recovery, the level of conversational restraint—along with any sense of dignity—took a nose dive directly into the floor.

"That old building probably hasn't had an electrical system update in decades. Dimes to dollars, that's what caused the fire." Mrs. Green nodded knowingly, as though she'd been a licensed electrician in a former life.

"Unless someone else started it. You know, on purpose." Mary whispered the last two words.

Mag and Clara opted to listen intently from the very edges of their lightly-padded, tweed-covered chairs. Bryer, the last of the town group to put forth a theory, opened his mouth to speak just as Perry Weatherall burst through the doors.

"Is Leanne all right? Evelyn said she was inside the office when the fire broke out."

Mag nodded, and Clara stood to pat Perry on the arm, "Yes, she's fine. And we made sure Max got out safely, too."

"Thank you," He leaned in close to keep from broadcasting his next statement to the entire waiting room, "I didn't want to admit to being worried about an animal while a human life hangs in the balance, but I'm grateful."

"Any word on how the fire started?" If the answer was anything other than arson, Clara knew someone was lying.

"Set." Perry pushed the word out between clenched teeth. "In the storage room. They tell me Bryer went in and saved Leanne. Stand-up guy, that one."

Dylan reemerged from the no-fly zone a few minutes later and began a detailed update on Leanne's condition, which included the joyous statement that she was awake and talking. Mag and Clara took full advantage of the distraction to slip into the hallway under another forbidden, heavy glamour.

"Might as well go straight to the top of the coven's naughty list. We've never been ones to do things halfway." Mag grinned with zero remorse as the pair hurried to Leanne's room, visiting hours and restrictions duly ignored.

"We're so sorry to barge in here like this, Leanne, but we're worried about you."

"If you're here, that means the fire was connected to Marsha's death, doesn't it?" Talking might have been a slight exaggeration. Leanne could hardly manage a croaking whisper.

"Well, dear," Clara's grandmotherly tone didn't match her youthful exterior but, since she actually *was* a grandmother, it smacked of authenticity when she said, "even if that weren't the case, we still would have checked in on you."

Thankfully, Leanne was so out of it, she probably wouldn't have batted an eyelash if Clara waved her wand and rode a broomstick around the room.

"Whoever started that fire could have killed you. Even if that wasn't the intention, this guy is obviously willing to go to the ends of the earth to hide something, and he doesn't care who gets caught in the crossfire. The hospital is secure"—Mag didn't mention that her confidence in that fact was due to the protective charm she'd surreptitiously placed on Leanne's room—"so you're not in danger here, but if you *are* a target, we need to act quickly."

"Why would I be a target?" she asked, plucking at the gleaming white sheet. "I have no idea why Marsha was killed."

"No, but it's possible you know *something*, even if you don't realize it. I know your throat is sore, but we need you to tell us what happened. Every detail you can remember, whether it seems significant or not."

Leanne attempted to shift into a more upright position, but in the process tugged on the line running from the crook of her arm into a bag of fluids hanging overhead. Clara helped her get situated, and was grateful that the woman was distracted enough not to notice that she was nearly naked with two practical strangers.

"Well, I couldn't sleep last night, so I decided to go into the office and clean up some details. We'd finalized and sent the commemorative edition out to the printers on Friday, and decided we'd skip the regular edition for this week. Everything was running so far behind, and I figured I could use the new printer and work up an insert." She paused, her lips tightening.

"I dug out some photos of Marsha, which were slated for a memorial spread, but when I got to the office and started leafing through them, it all came rushing back. Marsha's *I'm silently correcting your grammar* mug was still sitting on her desk right where she left it, and I couldn't stop the tears."

"That's when Perry found me in a puddle of my own snot. I think that crazy cat of his was probably yowling right along with me." She gasped and put her hand to her chest. "Oh, no, did Max get out all right?"

"Yes, yes, everyone else is fine, don't you worry." Clara patted Leanne's hand.

Leanne closed her eyes for a moment, her contorted face smoothing back to normal after a few deep breaths. "Anyway, I may have had a tiny breakdown, and sputtered on a bit about how things weren't going to be the same ever again, and how depressing it would be if the paper closed after all of Marsha's hard work. Perry told me not to worry, and that the paper would survive one way or another—Marsha had made sure of it—and I should mobilize the staff to prepare for some changes."

Mag and Clara waited patiently while Leanne skirted the events involving the actual fire, offering the expected oohs and ahhs when necessary to keep her calm.

"Did you see anyone else throughout the day? Talk to anyone, see anything suspicious?" Mag asked.

She thought for a minute, then shook her head. "No, but that's partly because I had the blinds drawn. It's like an oven in there when the sun beats in, and I forgot to open them again later. I never even unlocked the front door. I didn't realize how long I'd been there until the delivery truck showed up at the back door."

"You see, usually, we only get one box of each edition delivered to the office, but when we do a special, they're all stored in the back room, and we distribute them by hand." She let out a defeated sigh. "Of course, we won't be distributing this batch because they're all ruined, and there isn't time to have them reprinted."

"Anyway, Steve—the driver—helped me unload them into the hallway before he left. I got the boxes situated, closed the connecting door, and turned on my iPod while I finished the filing project I'd started earlier. A little while later, I smelled smoke and went out back to investigate. Stupidly, I opened the door"—Leanne held up a gauze-covered hand—"and burned myself in the process."

She lowered her hand back to the bed, twisting a little to accommodate the IV. "The smoke was like a wall, and the fire spread so fast. The front door was still locked, and I couldn't find my keys. I thought I was going to die in there. Then I heard sirens and felt myself being lifted up and carried outside. Those firefighters are going to be getting a huge gift basket, that's for sure."

"Actually, you were rescued by Bryer Mack, so you might want to funnel your thanks in his direction."

"Bryer? Really? And I always thought he didn't like me." Leanne made an attempt at lightheartedness that fell flat as she convulsed into a fit of ragged coughs.

Mag and Clara exchanged a look, agreeing they'd learned all they could and that it was time to take their leave.

"You rest, dear, and we'll be back to check on you tomorrow," Clara said as they left.

Chapter Thirteen

"The fliers are working, and they were a stroke of genius." Mag figured laying the praise on thick might net her an IOU from her sister—and she fully intended to cash in for something big, eventually.

Clara shrugged, "Thank Pye and Jinx. They were the ones who posted them all over town in the dead of night. The enchantment spell was a piece of cake. You know how I hate to interfere with free will, but what Hagatha did was worse. Anyone affected by the tainted merchandise will read the flier and be compelled to return to the shop, where we'll reverse Hagatha's spell and put an end to this madness. Anyone else will just see an ad for our sale—two birds, one stone."

A steady trickle of customers during the morning hours kept Mag and Clara both busy, and Clara noticed her sister couldn't keep the grin off her face as the cash register filled with bills of every denomination. But as the lunch hour approached, it became more and more difficult to maneuver around the growing swarm.

She wasn't sure how more people had managed to get the samples that were in the box, but she blamed Hagatha for that. If the old witch's goal had been to increase business—and Clara figured there was a good chance she'd had something else entirely in mind—she'd certainly succeeded.

The tale of Bryer Mack's daring rescue was the talk of the day, and Clara suspected a ticker-tape parade in his honor was forthcoming.

Not that she blamed them; Leanne's wan face was burned into her memory, and Clara was thankful Bryer had saved the woman who, she realized, was becoming a friend.

She was so lost in thought that she hadn't been paying attention to the chatter around her, but her ears perked when she picked up a particular conversation.

"I never would have expected it from him. Such an awkward boy, always covered with bruises. His mother said he could trip over his own shadow, but he's done well for himself." Mrs. Green delivered the proclamation with her typical elevated level of conviction, directing her comment toward anyone within earshot willing to engage in a good gossip session.

"What does one have to do with the other?" Mag mumbled in Clara's ear as she lumbered past the cash register with a box of Hagatha-free beauty products.

Clara grinned and tossed her a wink, "You read my mind."

"Essie Jones said it made her see him in a whole new light. She thought he was a geek in high school, but I saw her practically drooling as Bryer carried Leanne out of the building. And she wasn't the only one." One of the women amongst the group of Leanne's friends from the hospital waiting room piped up, wiggling her over-plucked eyebrows suggestively. Clara remembered she'd been named after some random color, but couldn't recall which one.

Another sort-of-familiar face answered Clara's question, "Well, Tawny, can you blame the women in this town? It's not as though we get a lot of fresh meat through here if you know what I mean. Sometimes, you have to shift your perspective in order to enjoy the view."

Several giggles followed, and when Clara caught Mag's eye from across the room, she knew her sister was running an internal dialog disparaging millennials, which to her, meant anyone under a solid century old. It occurred to her—not for the first time—that her sister had lost more than just her outward appearance. Take Gertrude Granger, for example: at least five hundred years beneath her Santa Claus-inspired gold buckled belt—twice Mag's age—and not even half as stodgy.

Something to do with the difference in attitudes. Gertrude saw the magic of Christmas sparkling over everything. Never mind that the secular side of the holiday rested outside the confines of witch traditions; Gertrude loved Santa and elves and toys and cookies and the rest of the whole shebang.

Mag, Clara was coming to realize, preferred a problem to dig into, a mystery to solve. But looking on the darker side of life for so long had biased her to believe the worst of people most of the time. And her focus on protecting others meant she spent too little time on herself. Something Clara vowed to rectify.

"Incoming," Mag muttered under her breath, sending the sentiment across the room to her sister on the wisp of a breeze.

Clara's head whipped toward the big bay window behind her, where Penelope, accompanied by Mabel and Evanora, marched up the front path in a beeline for the store entrance.

"Impeccable timing, of course." She rolled her eyes and returned her attention to a harried-looking customer waving an empty container of face cream. Holding up a hand, she said, "Ma'am, please relax, I promise I have plenty of stock in the back. Just hold on a moment, and I'll be right back."

The woman nodded her head several times in quick succession, trailing Clara to the rear stockroom door with desperation written all over her face.

Clara sighed, shot Mag an apologetic look, and disappeared into the recesses just as Penelope and company entered through the front, faces sour.

Bring it you hags, Mag thought to herself as she approached the trio with an excess of enthusiasm. "Hello, ladies. What can I help you find today? Perhaps some of Clara's miracle face cream? It's a hot seller."

Penelope's gaze zeroed in on Mag's face in an attempt to look intimidating, utterly failing against the unflappable Margaret Balefire.

"Is there somewhere we can speak privately?"

Choosing as secluded a corner as she could find, Mag dropped a dome of silence. Clara wouldn't appreciate it if Mag invited Penelope upstairs. Particularly if the woman continued to wear the I-smell-something-nasty look on her face.

"Do you think the coven invited you here to take advantage of the good people of Harmony? This is a clear violation of coven principles, and you two should be ashamed of yourselves. Using magic to boost sales is not just immoral, it's shameful. I expected more out of the famous Balefire sisters. Not much more, mind you, but the fact remains."

"With all due respect, Penelope, you have no idea what you're talking about. Clara's wares need no embellishment; if you want to burn someone at the stake, go find the old crow. Hagatha did this, and we're cleaning it up. If you'd like to help, please, by all means, go for it. Otherwise, we'll see you at the next coven meeting."

"How dare you flout the rules this way? How dare you?" Proving the need for the silencing spell, Penelope's voice took on the high-pitched tones of a restrained shriek.

"Me?" Mag barked, moving closer into Penelope's space. "How dare *you* restrict the right of every witch in the coven to live her life to the fullest of her magical potential? Blood witches live in every part of the world and have managed to conceal themselves without needing some tarted-up tramp to impose restrictions on them."

She took a breath, giving her words a second or two to sink in before continuing. "Look at Hagatha, for Hecate's sake. She's lived in this town since before it was a town, and no one seems to have noticed she's always been here. That's subtle magic. We were given these gifts to help, remember? Harm none, that's our way. The flip side of *harm none* is *helping all*. Don't you get that at all? Who raised you, anyway?"

"But I..." Inside the cone of silence, magic that had nothing to do with subtlety prickled along her skin and Penelope got a taste of what it meant to be on the bad side of a Balefire witch.

"But nothing," Mag said. "If you and your little playmates here can't handle yourselves in public..." Three sets of eyes decided shoes were more interesting than faces, and Mag finally clued in.

She crossed her arms and smirked. "Well, well, well. What was it? Love spell gone wrong? No, don't tell me. I'd rather let my imagination play with the visuals."

"It's what's best for the town. We all decided, and you can't go against the coven. Hagatha's already against us." Penelope shot back with less conviction than she'd previously displayed.

"How did you ever get her to agree to something like that in the first place?" Mag huffed through her nose. "You know what, I don't want to know."

"What are you going to do?" Penelope asked. "If you flout the rules the rest of the coven will do the same."

"And so they should. Witches were born to magic and sworn to use it responsibly."

With that, Mag dropped the spell, turned on her heel, and stalked into the back room where Clara was taking an inordinate amount of time packing a box to bring out front, especially considering she could have done it all with a snap of her fingers.

"Did I abuse you when we were children?" Mag demanded, glaring at Clara through a tuft of fluffy hair that had come loose during her huff. "Am I being punished for some long-forgotten transgression?"

"Sister dear, if I were punishing you, it would be for a recent and not-at-all-forgotten transgression. I simply provided you with an opportunity to grow as a person. The Mag I know would have gone all medieval on their badonkadonks." She scowled. "Fuzzy puppies! We've got to get her to break that no-cussing spell, or I might snap right along with you."

Chapter Fourteen

Velvet night settled over the town of Harmony like a balm, a full moon teasing silvered shadows out of the decorations readied for the upcoming festivities. Mounted on light poles, banner flags rustled in the gentle breeze.

Behind the closed doors and magically shuttered windows of Moonstone central, witches gathered to work on the final preparations.

Somewhere around dusk, the last of Mag's patience kissed her on the cheek and trotted merrily out the door. Without Clara to keep the peace, Penelope Starr might have earned a second taste of what it meant to be on the business end of a Balefire's wrath.

Not that Mag hadn't been provoked to the fine edge of reason and back by Penelope's doggedly superior attitude balanced by a complete lack of wits. Back in her bailiwick, she'd taken every opportunity to spout off about the no-magic rules while exhorting the witches to higher feats of it to get the rest of the tag-sale tables ready.

Double standards. Mag hated them.

Half an hour later, Penelope declared the Moonstones ready for the next morning, and since the rest of the town had long settled into their beds, she and her henchwomen took the instant route home. A wink, a blink, and they were gone, leaving Mag and Clara to lock up.

Shoulders lifting as if an enormous weight had dropped from them, Mag declared, "If she had shot her mouth off one more time, I was going to give her a new one on her butt." A flicker of witchfire dribbled sparks from the fist clenched at her side. "That woman does the two-step on my last nerve. And you're smiling. Do you find my pain amusing?"

"No. Of course, I don't. But I did enjoy the fact that ever since she returned from the ladies, she was flying the white flag."

"The what?" Mag didn't remember seeing any flag, or Penelope surrendering anything.

"The white flag," Clara repeated. "Toilet paper." She clarified when Mag missed the reference a second time. "Caught under her shoe."

Clara shook her head but smiled. "Sometimes your sense of humor would rival a twelve-year-old boy's, but lose out because it wasn't mature enough to compete."

One by one, the remaining coven members disappeared—each dimensional shift displacing enough air to make Mag's ears pop. Soon, only she and Clara remained behind to lock up.

"Go on ahead, I'm going to walk," Clara said. "I like the feel of moonlight on my face."

Mag looked at the clear, starry sky and shook her head. "No, I think I'll walk with you. Let the fresh air blow the stink of power-mad witch off me." She shrugged a lacy shawl, complete with fringe, over her shoulders.

Clara shot it a look of disdain. "Once this hoopla is over, we should skim back to Port Harbor and go clothes shopping. Not the second-hand shops, either. And maybe think about getting you a pair of jeans. This *Victorian grandmother meets*

128

flower child thing you've got going on is a little eccentric. We're business people now, you should dress the part."

"I don't like jeans. My lady parts—"

"Did you see that?" Grabbing Clara's arm and giving it a yank, Mag turned her to face the clock tower.

Clara was just thankful she didn't have to hear the end of that sentence because it might have scarred her for life. "No, I didn't see anything."

But then, she did. Moonlight glinted off something shiny at the base of the tower, flickered, and went out. Probably nothing, she thought, right up until strong magic prickled across her skin, raising every tiny hair to quivering attention.

"I think we'd better take a look."

On full alert, Margaret Balefire gave off a don't-mess-with-me vibe only an idiot would ignore. Or a high priestess with an agenda.

"Come to watch the preview?" Hagatha's voice creaked out of the shadow of the hydrangea bushes at the base of the clock tower. "It's going to be one hell of a show. They'll be talking about it for years."

Falling into the tone most people use with either the very young, very old, or someone who has strayed into the realm of the incurably wonky, Clara said, "Why, Hagatha, I can see you've certainly been up to something. We'd love a chance for a sneak peek."

Whether or not she saw through Clara's attempts to placate her, she was so eager to share her big plan that Hagatha practically danced in place—as much as anyone who needed a personal mobility aid could dance—and rubbed her hands together.

"Easier to show than tell." She snapped her fingers, and when dozens of candles flickered to life, the mystery of the great ulexite caper was solved. Chunks of the stone ringed the base of the clock tower, sparking in the light of the candles and the nearly full moon.

Amplified by Hagatha's abundant power, the fiber-optic qualities of the slices of stone created the perfect medium for a holographic show. So lifelike it was hard to tell the images were made from light and magic, the history of the clock tower played out in great detail.

A long, low whistle slid from Mag's lips. Old she might be, stubborn into the bargain, but Hagatha Crow had skills. "That's—"

"Better than a bunch of photos in a newspaper," Hagatha crowed. "It's almost like being there to see it in person."

She wasn't wrong. Both Mag and Clara felt compelled to step aside when they found themselves in the path of workers hauling in pieces of lumber to build scaffolding for the repairs done ten years before.

"It's fascinating," Clara said, meaning it. "Marvelous, really. But you know there's no way we can hide the existence of magic if the townspeople see this, right?"

"The magic-less never believe what's right in front of them. They'll think it's some new technology." Dismissing Clara's caution, Hagatha let out a cackling laugh. "See that? Look familiar? I'm the one who designed that float. Same as the one you built again this year. Penelope wouldn't recognize an original idea if it crawled up her leg and bit her on the ass."

"Hey!" Mag protested the use of forbidden slang by the very person responsible for the ban. "I thought you hated that kind of language. What about the charm on the house that twists my words every time I try to cuss? And while we're on the subject, I've tried everything except burning the place to the ground to break that."

While Mag pursued the subject of the anti-swearing charm, Hagatha's attention remained focused on adjusting the playback speed of her holographic event. Standing in the center of the square, she used her wand like a conductor. A flick of the wrist sped up the parade just enough to push it into the territory of high comedy. Another eased the speed back slightly to whittle the after party down to a spare few minutes, and when it was over, she clapped her hands to end the show.

"Imagine the applause." In a surprisingly graceful motion, Hagatha curtsied. How her ancient knees let her bend so deeply seemed like a miracle.

"It's a little premature to be taking your bows before the story ends, isn't it?" Having been shut down on lifting the cussing ban, Mag let the question turn into a sneer.

"I don't know what you're—" So rarely did Hagatha experience an event she couldn't anticipate that the flickering image of a young woman standing on the balcony under the belly of the clock shocked her into silence.

A shining wing of blond hair swung around a heart-shaped face made more remarkable by her smile. The woman stepped up onto the railing, wrapped an arm around the narrow column, and leaned out over the square.

Clara's heart kicked against her ribcage at the reckless sight.

"She's going to fall."

But she didn't. The shining beauty executed a perfect pivot around the pole and landed safely at the edge of the clock's shadow. There was no audio, but there didn't need to be. The twitch of her shoulders, the abrupt way she froze in place was all it took to know someone had entered the tower.

Tension settled into narrow shoulders as slim hands lifted to paint the air with sharp gestures. She spun away once, presented an angry expression to the dumbfounded witches below, then turned back to continue arguing.

The next part happened fast, like a blur. The blond took an angry step into the shadows, and then she was falling backward. The railing caught just below her center of balance, and she flipped over to plummet toward the ground.

Clara turned away to keep from seeing the gruesome impact, but Mag's attention stayed trained on the tower where one shadow moved dark against the rest. Anticipation settled over her as the chin and jawline of a face came into view. A man, a boy really—she could tell by the softness of the curve—but that was all she saw before he retreated and the magic image sparked and fizzled into darkness.

"I knew it. I knew it." Hagatha chortled. "Been saying for years someone got away with murder that night and no one ever believed batty old Haggie."

"Did you see who it was? Run it again and let it go another few minutes, would you?"

"Can't. Takes time to regenerate. Won't be ready to play again until the final showing tomorrow night. See you then, ladies." Hagatha took herself off, presumably to her niece's house. Word had it she'd taken over the run of the place, and the niece was now living in a potting shed. But rumors can often become exaggerated in small towns.

Chapter Fifteen

Once the square was quiet again, Mag looked at Clara with resignation. "It pains me to dismantle some of the finest spell work I've ever seen. If not for the nasty ending, I'd be tempted to let it play out."

Stepping into the shadows, Clara conjured a wheelbarrow and started tossing in the charmed stones Hagatha had hidden around the base of the clock tower. If she agreed with Mag, she was careful not to let on.

"What on earth is going on over here?" The voice of Gertrude Granger coming out of the darkness sent Clara's heart lurching.

"Good goddess, you scared a year off my life, Gertrude," she said, clutching her chest as her heartbeat returned to normal. "What brings you back so late at night?"

"I felt the magic building and figured I'd better come and check just to make sure Hagatha wasn't up to something."

"She was, but we put a stop to it. Was she always like this? It seems like she's hellbent on exposing herself, and us by extension, to the town of Harmony. Did something set her off?"

Bending to help lift a sizable chunk of the stone, Gertrude grunted, and Clara wasn't sure if from effort or from the question.

"There was an incident that could have led to the harm of an innocent, and Penelope decided that the only way to keep it from happening again would be to stop doing magic in public at all. She lobbied, and while we don't run a coven like a democracy, exactly, it turned into a rule. Hagatha rebelled and keeps rebelling, and that's how you ended up here."

As the pair of them rounded the third corner of the tower, Clara described the elderly witch's latest caper and couldn't quite keep the admiration from her voice.

"We saw that poor girl die and it was no accident." Mag rejoined them.

Gertrude tossed another stone in the wheelbarrow with a clatter. "You really didn't know that Marsha wasn't the first woman in town to die of suspiciously accidental circumstances, did you? You've been here a few months now; I can't believe you haven't heard the story of Blossom Von Gunten."

Gertrude dropped the bomb as innocuously as if she were sprinkling seedlings into a pot of soil—with similar effect, considering the rate at which realization sprouted and bloomed into something resembling understanding.

"Von Gunten, Von Gunten—where have I heard that name before? It's not a common name." Mag searched her memory, her eyes darting back and forth until realization dawned and she and Clara both spoke at the same time. "From Marsha!"

"She mentioned an Aldo Von Gunten the day we met her. He was the expert who restored the tower clock to its former glory."

"And she started to tell us that something happened to his daughter."

"Sounds like you had a front row seat for what happened to his daughter, a tragedy that rocked the whole town." Gertrude intoned.

"Well, stop beating around the bush and tell us what you know." Mag sent the wheelbarrow full of stones to the safety of her backyard.

"Come back to the house for a cup of cocoa, and we'll talk," Gertrude said.

With a pop, they landed in the shadows at the edges of Gertrude's yard. Refusing to answer more questions until safely ensconced, she strode out of the entryway and into the bowels of her very merry house, leaving the sisters to follow as she made her way to the parlor.

She settled onto a tufted armchair next to the flickering flame of Balefire every witch keeps burning in her hearth all year round. The elf-obsessed witch paused for dramatic effect until the steam pouring out of Mag's ears went from proverbial to literal.

"Blossom Von Gunten was just about the prettiest girl I'd ever seen—and I'd say she had one of the sweetest dispositions as well. I watched her grow up from a babe, as I have watched every person in this town be born, live their life, and die for a very long time now. But Blossom was different. Selfless, innocent, and kind don't begin to describe that girl."

She blew on her cocoa and took a sip, staring into the Balefire. "Only child she was, and no mother to speak of. Followed her father around everywhere. Right little tomboy, though she looked like a princess. Always climbing around up in the clock tower—so dangerous—and everyone warned her that one day she'd fall to her death. Didn't stop her from climbing though."

Gertrude shook her head, the faraway look clearing. "Anyway, like so many young people, she wanted more than what Harmony had to offer, so Blossom worked hard and won a scholarship to some fancy ivy-league college. And then, like so many slightly less young people, she learned that sometimes, your home really is where your heart belongs."

"Of course," she said with a wistful smile, "it didn't hurt that she'd met a nice young man who wanted to marry her, settle down, have babies, and raise them someplace quiet, in a sleepy little town just like this. She came back, as they so often do. Although, this time I sorely wish she hadn't. Maybe things would have turned out differently, and Blossom might have had the life she deserved."

Clara and Mag listened with rapt attention, their cocoas going cold.

"I remember clear as day—the Circle had gone all-out in preparation for the bicentennial celebration, and though Mr. Von Gunten had achieved great fame as a restoration expert, he certainly didn't have a lot to show for it when it came to money. Once we'd closed up for the night, most of the town pitched in to transition the decorations into something suitable for a low-budget wedding. That's how many lives Blossom had touched."

"I know what you're thinking," Gertrude raised an eyebrow at Mag's unhidden eye roll.

"People glorify the dead—forget they had faults just like the rest of us still among the living—but in this case, I assure you if Blossom had any skeletons in her closet, they were of the inflatable sort you see during October. The next morning, her body was found on the front steps. It was ruled an accident, though the police conducted a thorough investigation. Hogwash if you ask me, not that anyone ever did."

"Why didn't you speak up, then? And why didn't you try to figure out who the killer was?"

"Haven't you ever heard that old expression about not meddling in the affairs of mortals? When you've seen as much as I have, you learn that there's a circle of life. Where would I draw the line? You two were invited here because one of us became embroiled in the world of normals and set off a skirmish that came close to breaking up our coven. Having truck with humans is fraught with danger."

A sharp crack sounded when Mag banged her mug on the table.

"Don't even get me started on how a clash of egos rendered it necessary to call in outside help for your coven. Or how ludicrous it is for Hagatha to engage in a role reversal to make a point. We're here now, and caught in the middle, but at least now we know what the sides are all about. All of that pales when there's a young woman who has gone without justice far too long, and you could have done something about it." Mag's face was red with outrage.

"Piffle." Gertrude snorted. "If I got involved with every wrongdoing I saw, I'd never get anything else done. Besides, what was I going to say? *My witchly intuition tells me someone murdered this girl. I don't know who or why, but you should look into that?"*

She waved a dismissive hand. "You must have noticed the law enforcement in this town is sorely lacking imagination—and it's been like that for as long as I can remember. When you've lived here as long as I have, you'll learn to ignore coincidences like two women falling to their deaths ten years apart."

Before Mag's head exploded, Clara intervened and dragged them both out of there, thanking Gertrude for the cocoa.

On the short walk home, Mag postulated, "There it is again, Clarie, that word *coincidence*. Two murdered women; the same MO, in the same small town. There has to be a connection."

"I agree. We've looked at Marsha's death from every possible angle, and it's pretty clear we're missing something. Maybe it's time to shift our perspective."

"Exactly. Maybe if we solve Blossom's murder, we'll solve Marsha's as well. Two birds, one stone."

Clara's nostrils flared, "Nice choice of words, Maggie."

Mag ignored the admonishment, her mind racing ahead. "Marsha must have known something she wasn't supposed to know. The question is whether she went looking or stumbled onto the evidence."

"You think she figured out who the murderer is?"

"Maybe, or maybe she was on the right track. Either way, she got close, which is good for us because that means there's evidence, and maybe even proof somewhere." Mag looked positively thrilled at the prospect.

"But we've got to begin at the beginning—investigate Blossom's death, and then see where it meets up with Marsha's."

Chapter Sixteen

"You doing okay, Maggie?" Loathe to admit the slope was stealing her breath, Clara used her sister as an excuse for a short rest. Or tried to, anyway. It had been her idea to combine the trip to visit Aldo Von Gunten with a bit of morning exercise, so complaining about the workout wouldn't fly with Mag.

"I'm fine. Ain't the uphill that bothers me; it's going to be the return trip that does me in. If we're going to mostly live like non-magical folk, we should use the van more often."

"The exercise is good for you. You have to admit your mobility is much improved. And isn't your new life better than the way you were living in the Fringe? Sitting in some grungy hovel made out of sticks and feeling sorry for yourself?"

Looks don't kill, not even magical ones, but Clara felt the heat and sting of her sister's glare.

Von Gunten lived in a tidy Dutch colonial about two-thirds of the way up Turner Street. His meticulously painted front porch faced an impressive view of the town and the clock tower. Having witnessed Blossom's last moments the night before, Clara's soft heart felt a pang for the man who faced the sight of both a personal triumph and his greatest tragedy on a daily basis.

While she mused over that sad thought, Mag rapped her knuckles briskly against the leaded-glass panel of the front door and listened for a response. There was none. Not right away, at least, and before she had time to knock again, the clock struck the hour.

Noon meant a solid dozen peals of the bell, every one of which was echoed by a chorus of chimes and cuckoos coming from inside the house.

"They'd be carting me off to the funny farm inside of a week if I had to listen to that racket every day. Do you think they all go off like that around the clock?" Mag muttered.

Mercifully, since the Balefires now lived within hearing distance of the big bells, there was a mechanism in place that stilled the hammer from nine o'clock in the evening until nine in the morning. Even so, Mag vowed she would eventually be forced to put the kibosh on the bell, or she might be tempted to kill someone.

"I'd assume so. Seems reasonable to me that a clock-maker might want to have—oh, I don't know—*clocks* in his house." Sometimes Mag's carping got on Clara's nerves.

And so, if for no other reason than to curtail a diatribe, she nudged her sister aside and rapped more firmly on the glass. "Mr. Von Gunten, are you there? We'd like to speak to you for a moment."

"Hold your horses, I'm coming." The thick panel muffled his voice, but Clara saw the shape of someone moving through the patterned glass. "Who's there?"

"Well, my name is Clara, and I'm here with my mother, Margaret. We'd like to ask you a few questions about—I'm sorry to say—but about your daughter. If you wouldn't mind."

The door opened, but barely a crack, and at that moment, it occurred to Clara they hadn't thought this through before making the trek up the hill. Asking questions about his daughter's death would be painful at best, and awkward to boot.

"Was there anyone who might want to—" Mag got no further before Clara trod heavily on her foot, but she took the hint and fell silent.

"May we come in, please?" Even to Clara, the smile on her face felt full of false cheer.

"Don't know you, don't want to talk about Blossom, don't see any reason why I should let you traipse through my place."

"I'm sorry for intruding, but I have to ask." Trying to frame it more delicately than her sister would have done, Clara said, "Was there ever any doubt your daughter's death happened by accident?"

What little bit of his face that showed through the crack between the frame and the door went pale. "I never thought Blossom would fall. Not after all the hours she spent with me while I worked. Can't tell why you'd want to dredge this all up now, after so many years, but if you want to know who had a reason to hurt my girl, go talk to that ex-boyfriend of hers."

The door shut firmly in their faces, and the clicking of the lock put an exclamation point on the dismissal.

"Would have been nice if he'd bothered to give us a name." Grumpy about the futility of the trip, Mag stomped down the steps while Clara pulled out her phone.

"We should have asked Gertrude for more details, but a tragedy like that in a town this size would have been covered in the paper and even in the statewide news outlets. Shouldn't take me more than a minute to find something."

While Clara's fingertip whizzed across the touch screen, Mag's annoyance translated itself into the staccato tap of her cane on the sidewalk.

"You're going to be staring down at that thing and fall in a well one of these days," she grumbled.

"If I do, I'm sure Lassie will alert Timmy, and he'll find you to save the day. And I've found it." Clara let out a long, low whistle. "You're never going to guess who Blossom's fiancé was. Come on, give it a go."

"If I wanted to play twenty questions, I'd go find a child. Just tell me."

"Dylan Snow. Isn't that an interesting coincidence?"

"Dylan Snow? Leanne's husband." Picking her way slowly down the steepest part of the hill, Mag fell to silent contemplation while Clara continued to read.

Three-quarters of the success of a good spell came down to the witch's ability to visualize the outcome in meticulous detail. Mag tapped into that skill now.

In her mind's eye, she cast images of the key players against a blank wall. Marsha, Leanne, Dylan, Perry, and Blossom ranged in a loose circle around the edges. After another moment's thought, she added a hazy silhouette in the center with a question mark for a face.

Like a game of connect-the-dots, she drew a green line between Marsha and every other person on the board except for Blossom, who got a red line until the connection between the two women could be established. For all Mag knew they'd never met.

Using blue this time, she created lines leading from Dylan to both Blossom and Leanne. The two women were linked with yellow, but no obvious pattern pointed to a clear suspect.

"If there's a connection between the two deaths, I can't see it," she finally admitted. "Why now? Blossom's killer got away with murder because no one was looking at her death as anything other than an accident. History seems to be repeating itself with Marsha. That's too big a coincidence to ignore, and it points to the same killer both times. Stick with what you know, right? But why now? That's the question that keeps coming back to haunt me. We need to talk to someone who was around for both murders."

"Someone from the coven, you mean?" Clara asked. "Not Hagatha, I hope. She's about as trustworthy as a kid with her hand already in the cookie jar, and I think Gertrude told us all she knew. Honestly, that woman could be standing on the tracks and not notice the train unless it was covered in tinsel."

"Or smelled like gingerbread." At the bottom of the hill now, Mag made a beeline for one of the benches dotting the verge between the sidewalk and the wrought iron fence on the corner and tossed in her agreement. "But no. I was thinking about Dylan."

"So you're leaning toward it being him? He would have a brass set on him if he stuck around for ten years only to commit the same crime the same way a second time. He didn't strike me as the type to be carrying heavy artillery." Ripe skepticism flowed off Clara in waves. Only someone brutally ruthless or monumentally stupid would pull a trick like that, and she didn't think Dylan fit either of those descriptions. "I can't see it."

Mag scowled at her. "As a source of information is what I meant. He would not be on the top of my suspect list—if I had a suspect list. How are we supposed to solve a decade-old murder when there are no clues or evidence? It was easier hunting Raythes—they're evil, but they're upfront about it."

Dylan Snow looked like he hadn't gotten an iota of decent sleep in days, not that either of the Balefire sisters could blame him. With Leanne still admitted to the hospital, he'd been trekking back and forth and spending most of his time on an uncomfortable fold-out chair that served—though barely qualified—as a bed.

143

Clara decided they'd marched up to enough practical strangers' houses over the last few days, people were going to start wondering if they were part of some kind of door-to-door pyramid scheme.

This time, at least, the occupant didn't look disappointed when he opened the door. "Hello, Mrs. And, er, Ms. Balefire."

Clara smiled, "Just Mag and Clara are fine, Dylan."

"Did you come here to check up on Leanne? She's not here. They haven't released her yet, but she's doing well. I wanted to thank you for that basket of mini muffins you sent to the hospital. So much better than anything they have in the cafeteria. Leanne and I are both glad you two decided to move to Harmony."

"You're more than welcome," Clara answered. "Actually, we came to talk to you."

"Really? What about?"

Clara ran through the usual spiel that was becoming quite familiar, and, ignoring his insistence they had to be mistaken, caught Dylan up to speed. "So, as you can see, we need your help."

"Well," he said, "to be honest, Blossom's death isn't a subject I'd like to discuss with virtual strangers. It was the worst thing that has ever happened to me, and considering how stressful my life has been lately, the last thing I want to do is relive it."

Clara opened her mouth to say something respectful, and let Dylan off the hook, but it was Mag's turn to put in her two cents, and there was no way she was leaving without having some questions answered.

"You dated Blossom for what, a couple of years in college?" she asked with an edge in her voice. "What about her father, her friends? They spent many more years loving her. Don't they deserve the closure we could give them? And

144

what about Marsha Hutchins? She was your friend as well, wasn't she? Don't you want to bring their killer to justice?"

He raked his fingers through his hair. "Look, of course, I want that, I'm not an animal. It's just that there's not much I can tell you. I only moved to Harmony to be with Blossom. I stayed because at first, it was enough to feel her presence—to walk the same streets she walked, experience the life she wanted for us. And then when Leanne and I—well, the point is, even though I wondered if there was more to Blossom's death, there was never any evidence of foul play."

The shaky quality of Dylan's voice revealed the doubt he felt—that everyone who was close to Blossom seemed to feel—about the nature of her death. It amazed Clara that people—witch or human, it didn't make any difference in these types of situations—could ignore their instincts and accept something they otherwise would reject, simply because someone with a badge told them to.

And therein lay the difference between the two Balefire sisters: cut from the same cloth, their life experiences varied vastly. Mag's had taught her that the mind is capable of creating a protective barrier against unwelcome information. Which for some, was a blessing rather than the curse her sister presumed it to be.

"We're not asking you for proof; we're just asking for your opinion."

"It's not my opinion you need," Dylan shook his head sadly, "It's Leanne's. She was Blossom's best friend. If anyone has inside information to share, it will be her."

Chapter Seventeen

"I call driver this time, Clarie. I feel the need to put the pedal to the metal."

"That doesn't bode well for me, I don't think, but go for it."

They hustled down the hill, hopped into the VW bus, and managed to shave five minutes off their arrival time thanks to Mag's lead foot.

Mag beamed with pride when she noticed the protection charm on Leanne's hospital room was still intact. "Can we come in?" She asked, poking her head in through the cracked door.

"Yes, of course." Leanne beckoned them inside, her voice nearly back to normal and her color improved.

"You look much better, they must be releasing you soon," Clara commented while fluffing Leanne's pillow.

"Yes, tomorrow actually. I can't wait to get home; I can't handle any more soap operas, and the hospital only has basic cable. I'm going a little bit batty." Clara, who had a DVR full of Days of Our Lives at home, declined to comment. "Now, is this a social call, or have you figured out what happened to Marsha?"

"Not yet, but we're getting closer—and what we've discovered is that her murder might have something to do with the death of Blossom Von Gunten. We're very nearly certain the two are related."

Leanne's eyes widened in surprise and an undercurrent of pain that set a single tear hovering on her lashes, "Whatever in the world are you talking about? Are you saying…what I think you're saying?" Something in her tone caught Mag's attention.

"You don't seem particularly shocked by the idea. Why don't you tell us about what happened back then? We know you two were best friends, and we know Dylan was going to marry Blossom. What we don't know is, who would have had a reason to kill her?"

Leanne accepted Clara's proffered tissue and took a moment to clean herself up. "Nobody, as far as I'm concerned. But nothing would shock me at this point, and honestly, in some strange way, I always felt like there was something off about her death. For more than the obvious reason that she could tiptoe across a balance beam as lightly as a feather—we had been closer than sisters for our entire lives. I'll tell you my story, and maybe you can help us lay this all to rest.

"Blossom and I shared the terrible fate of having lost a mother early in life. Neither of us remembered ours, and we were both raised by our fathers. Daddy always said he felt Mama's presence the day he met Aldo over at Darby's. Two sad men with baby girls at home—they bonded immediately, and the two of us grew up together.

"Of course, we had our differences like all girls do, particularly considering how beloved Blossom was. She shined so brightly, and I faded into the shadows. Which was okay with me, up to a certain point. Watching her be crowned homecoming queen, prom queen, and basically, the princess of Harmony stung a little, sure.

147

"We were teenagers; of course, I felt jealous. But you couldn't stay mad at Blossom for long. She could have used her popularity to snag the captain of the football team for a boyfriend, but instead, she chose Bryer Mack who, in high school, was as close to a nobody as a guy could get. He was part of the chess and AV clubs, so far below Blossom's station that I think he felt like an angel was smiling down on him when she showed an interest.

"They dated all through school, but then Blossom took that scholarship and Bryer stayed here to help out on his dad's farm. It was a quiet breakup, and when she returned after college with Dylan by her side, Bryer was gracious and congratulatory. I remember thinking how lucky she was— even when she broke someone's heart, they practically thanked her for it. Like just knowing her, having been in her presence for a little while, was enough of a gift.

Her mouth twisted into a wry smile. "Funny, how true that statement turned out to be. Nobody got to keep her. And that's how Dylan and I ended up together. I certainly didn't set out to marry my best friend's fiancé, but sometimes that's just how things work out. Shared grief creates a bond, and from that bond, we built a real relationship."

She lifted a hand. "Don't get me wrong; there are moments where I'll catch him wearing a wistful expression, and I wonder if he's thinking about her. She'll always be the young, beautiful girl she was when she died—her boobs won't get saggy, and she'll never get crow's feet or cellulite, or become an old lady. In a way, I envy her as much now as I did then."

No wonder Leanne chased perfection with such dogged determination, Clara thought sadly.

"Blossom's death never *did* set well with me. At the time, I blamed it on emotions like shock and anger and self-pity. I dreamed she came back, over and over; it had all been a lie,

148

and she wasn't dead at all. After a while, time washed over those feelings, smoothing their edges like the ocean beating against the sand. And then I started to wonder if perhaps there was more to it.

"Blossom loved spending time up in that clock tower, and the scholarship she received was for gymnastics, of all things. Of course, accidents happen all the time, and it's certainly within the realm of possibility. But I spent that entire day with Blossom, and when I left her, she said she wanted to climb up and look down on Harmony one last time as a single woman."

Along with an onslaught of silent tears, mascara tracked down Leanne's face leaving a black, blotchy mess in its wake.

"I got the idea she was out for something more like quiet contemplation, and goofing around up there didn't seem like part of her agenda. But accidents happen, and we all had to accept she was gone."

"And everything was hunky dory with Dylan? How did he react to the idea of living in the same town as her ex-boyfriend?" Mag asked when Leanne was finished with her tale. "They must have run into Bryer at some point."

"My husband is not a killer. He's so gentle with me, with his children. I would know if he had that kind of darkness in him." Leanne's conviction took the form of cold, hard truth and burning-hot defense.

"Blossom and Dylan were *that* couple. The one everyone loves to hate because they're so perfect together they make you look at your own relationship with a critical eye. Sometimes I wonder if they'd have held it together for the long term."

She raised a brow. "Call me skeptical, but that kind of perfection never lasts. He was so besotted by Blossom I doubt he even noticed Bryer existed. After all, he'd won her heart and Bryer wasn't even a blip on his radar. They're friends

149

now, you know," she mused. "I wonder if they ever talk about her when I'm not around."

"What about Bryer Mack? Did he have the opportunity?"

"No. He had the sense to leave before the wedding, so he wasn't even in town when Blossom died. He said he'd been planning that road trip for months, but I think he thought it would be awkward to watch her marry another guy. He tooled out of here on his motorcycle two days before the wedding, and when he got back and found out what happened, he was distraught. But then, so was everyone.

Blossom's poor father—you know, I still visit him, but we never talk about her. Nobody does. It's always seemed such a shame. When Marsha started putting together the commemorative edition, she wanted to feature a story about Blossom, but I managed to talk her into nixing it in favor of a photograph and reprint of the obituary. She was always fascinated by what happened, and she asked a lot of questions. Maybe she asked the wrong person the wrong question."

A memory flitted across Mag's consciousness; something she couldn't quite put her finger on, but that insisted on being explored. "It's to do with what went in that paper. That's the only explanation. Marsha had those photos remastered— photos from the very same day Blossom died. There must have been something in one of them that the murderer didn't want anyone to see!"

"And that's why he burned the papers when they came. Leanne, please tell us you have a copy left somewhere?" Clara implored.

Leanne shook her head sadly, "I don't. But the printers might. I can call them on Monday."

Looking at Leanne's pale face and the angry red marks on her arms, Mag's instincts screamed that if getting Leanne out of the way had been his goal, the killer might try to find a way to finish the job. Her protections charm might not be enough to sway the mind of a murderer with only one goal.

"Monday isn't good enough. There's got to be another way." Mag's statement was meant for her sister, but Leanne, having suddenly remembered something of importance, was the one to answer.

"The negatives! Marsha put them in the fire safe, but the fire department hasn't let anyone back in."

"You leave that part to us."

Chapter Eighteen

The acrid stink of wet and blackened wood layered over smoke caught in Clara's throat, crawled down into her belly, and set it churning as she made her way to the fire safe in the Harmony Holler office. In the clear light of day, she saw how the aftermath of the fire had gutted the place, turned it into a post-apocalyptic nightmare of slagged plastic and twisted metal.

Her memory overlaid an image of the newspaper office as she had seen it on that first day, and she wished she'd paid more attention to the photos then.

"Negatives. It had to be negatives. That's what? Two weeks minimum to get back prints, even if we put a rush on the order." Clara grabbed the knob and tried to give the dial a spin, but soot and debris clogged the mechanism. She tried again. And again while Mag smirked until Clara groaned in defeat.

"It's no use, it won't open."

"You really do take the personal-use thing a step too far." Sparks arced between Mag's crooked finger and the dial, which coughed out a cloud of dust and spun free. "What's the good in having a gift if you never use it?"

"Okay, Hagatha lite. Point made. Now help me get this open." The closet-sized safe door turned out to be a lot lighter than it looked.

"What is this thing made out of?" Only Mag's tight grip on her cane kept her from overbalancing. Inside the safe, floor to ceiling shelves held dozens of narrow boxes, each one labeled with the year. "Look, they stop after 2005. Isn't that odd?" She reached for the box they had come here to find. "What do you suppose happened to the rest of them?"

"I keep forgetting you missed the technological revolution. That must have been the first year they went digital. But there should still be some sort of media storage. What did they call them again? Flip flops?"

"What do shoes have to do with it? Modern technology is your thing; I prefer the simple life."

"Oh, like before there was fire or the wheel? Or the refrigerator? How would you keep your ice cream frozen?" While she scoffed, Clara's mind supplied the proper term from her research into the advancements made during her stony period. "Floppies. There should be floppies, or disks, or thumb drives somewhere. Then again, Leanne didn't know if Marsha was using the cloud for the remastered images."

"Do you have any idea how ridiculous all of that sounds? Floppies and driving thumbs. How do clouds figure in? Never mind. I don't want to know."

Mag rifled through the contents but found nothing fitting the bill.

"It looks like we're stuck with old-fashioned methods. With all the modern advancements, there must be a faster way to get prints from negatives."

"Well, there *was* a phenomenon called one-hour photo processing. Every drug store in the country had it. No more waiting weeks for photos. Now, since hardly anyone uses film anymore, those have gone out of style, and it's back to sending out for prints. You know, all in the name of progress because film has become obsolete." That much she'd seen for herself over the years.

Human drug stores drew Mag like fruit flies to a ripe melon. All the little bottles of this and that and the pills. Oh, the pills. Tablets and capsules with tiny, sterile beads rattling around inside, yellows and blues and reds. Mag collected pills, and if she had resorted to magical means to get them, she'd never tell.

"Ah, Maggie, sometimes I feel obsolete, too." Clara lost herself in a moment of silent thought, then picked up the box of negatives, shoved the safe door closed, and spun the lock.

Back at Balms and Bygones, an hour of tapping away at computer keys armed Clara with enough knowledge to set up a darkroom. If she were going to do this at all, she'd do it her way—using a blend of magic and whatever she had to hand.

"Sorry," Clara grimaced when a small, pewter cauldron nearly cleaned her sister's clock as it sped from the shelf to her work table. Grinning, Mag settled back to watch Clara work.

A thumb-sized chunk of ulexite went quickly to powder in the unforgiving spot between mortar and pestle. To that, she added a dash of mercury, a few flakes of silver, several herbs, and enough of Mag's high-octane moonshine to thin the mixture out. Three drops of pigment ink swirled into the shining liquid, and then she swung the cauldron into the Balefire where it came to a bubble in a matter of seconds.

"Here we go." She ladled a shimmering puddle onto a sheet of paper. For a second or two, nothing happened, and Clara forgot to breathe, but then the blob spread out, and the paper sucked it in with an audible pop. This she repeated six more times.

154

"And now, for step two." Craning her head sharply, Clara simply looked at each window to turn them an inky black, and soon there was no other light in the room, save for the fire crackling on the hearth. She selected a strip of negatives and blessed whoever had organized them with date, time, and subject matter.

"Why did you make it dark? The paper's already been exposed to light." Curiosity drove Mag's question, not criticism. Despite herself, she'd done a fair amount of peeking over Clara's shoulder during the research phase, and the process carried enough alchemy to interest her.

"Reducing the chance of phantom images showing up. This next part is going to take both of us. Can you hold the negative perfectly steady above the papers? I'm going to try to print the whole strip at once."

With a snort to indicate the request was child's play, Mag sent a solid flow of magic to the strip of negatives. They rose and froze into place.

"Perfect, and now for the light." Because it was both the closest and the most controllable source, Clara scooped up a handful of magical Balefire.

"I think white will work best." With a little concentration, yellow and orange tongues of flame went white as the purest driven snow.

"Hold steady now." The power banked inside of Clara flared to life, and so did the ball of fire she held. She tipped her hand over to beam magical light through the negative and onto the paper.

"Didn't work," Mag announced and wafted the negatives back onto the table next to the blank pieces of paper. "There's bound to be a one-hour photo place left somewhere in the northern hemisphere. Get me a landmark to target, and I'll get there and back without being seen."

155

"Your faith in me is simply astounding." Clara's tone was so dry it could suck the moisture out of the air. With a sharp series of motions, she scooped up the sheets, flicked a bobbing ball of red witchfire to hang over the sink, and twisted the taps.

After adjusting and testing the water temperature for long enough to elicit an impatient sound from Mag, Clara slid the first sheet of paper gently into the clear stream and watched the image appear as if rinsed onto the paper.

"Hah! Vindicated." Clara sent the newly-formed image toward the fireplace for drying and started working her way through the stack. When the final sheet hung in midair near the heat, she released her spell on the windows to let a flood of light into the room, then began to inspect the pictures with a critical eye.

"Out of focus. Wrong angle. Is that Penelope? Not a good look for her. Wait, this one's better. And we have a winner." Snagging the dry photo, Clara sent the rest into the fireplace. "It's crisp—I added some ginkgo to the brew for clarity." Still, she squinted as she scanned for clues.

"Let me see that," Mag made a grab for the photo. "Let's do this right." Laying her thumb and index finger close together against the paper, she made a flicking motion and slid them apart. The photo blew up to the size of a bed sheet and hovered in the center of the room.

"You've seen me do that with my phone, copycat."

"Just imagine how nice it would be if you could do that with other things."

"Ew, are you trying to put dirty thoughts in my head? Because if you are, it worked. And now I need at least a gallon of brain bleach."

"Gutterbrain, I was talking about ice cream."

"Forget about that! I found Blossom and Dylan," Clara pointed. "Doesn't look like there was any friction there at all—see her posture? Straight spine, a little flirt in her shoulders and the tilt of her head. And they're leaning into each other."

"Mmpf," Mag acknowledged. "There's Leanne draped all over some young fellow. Looks like a cat in heat. Could be trying to make Dylan jealous? Maybe she had a thing for him all along. We've ruled her out for Marsha, but she could have done Blossom."

"It's the makeup, right?" Presenting a raised eyebrow, Clara assessed Mag's willingness to doubt Leanne even now.

"She wears it like a mask, and you only wear a mask if you're trying to hide something. What do you think that is?"

"Didn't you ever fall in love, Maggie? I know this falls into the realm of things we never talk about, but that realm is worlds too big. It feels like I hardly know anything about you at all. Every time I ask you anything, you throw up a wall and—don't you dare shake your head at me! You're doing it right now when all I want to know is if you were ever happy like that. Was there ever anyone special?"

"There's more to life than putting on war paint and shaking your—" Hagatha's no-cursing charm slapped into effect. "Argh!" Mag pointed to her breasts and her behind with an exaggerated motion. "Around for the attention of someone who will tell you pretty lies and then leave because you don't look like a teenager anymore."

"So there was someone, and you do understand why Leanne feels like she's always been measured and found wanting. She trowels on the makeup in an attempt to retain youth while you went the other way and elevated personal crankiness to an art form."

"Whatever." Deflecting was another of Mag's strong suits. "I still think there could be something there."

"Look where they are, though. There's no possible line of sight between Leanne and Blossom or Dylan from that spot. No way she's trying to make him jealous by hiding behind the rose bushes where he can't see her rubbing up against someone else. If that's what you're selling, I'm not buying."

"Fine. Then who does that leave? In case you haven't noticed, we've run out of suspects unless you think her old man shoved Blossom off that balcony."

Clara didn't, but the mention of Blossom's father clicked a switch in her head, and the light of understanding came on bright.

"The father sent us to Dylan, but what exactly was it he said? Do you remember?"

"Go talk to her fiancé."

"Boyfriend. He said boyfriend, not fiancé."

"Whoop-de-doo," Mag deadpanned. "Same difference."

"Oh, no it isn't. He was talking about someone else entirely—he was talking about Bryer Mack." Clara began scanning the enormous photograph to see if she could pick out another familiar face.

The dominoes fell, but Mag shrugged it off. "Bryer wasn't in town the day Blossom died. Leanne said he was out of—" she cut off abruptly when her sister let out a whoop and did a happy dance that included a lot of jiggling flesh and a beaming smile.

"I found it. Look, do you notice anything familiar?"

"What? Hold still long enough so I can see where you're pointing."

"There. Right there." Clara pointed to something partially hidden on the shadowed side of the building. "Look familiar?"

The 1977 Kawasaki KZ1000, partially covered by hydrangeas, carried a familiar license plate.

BRYGUY

Chapter Nineteen

"Looks like we found the missing link. Bryer killed Blossom and let everyone think it was an accident until Marsha sent those photos out for digital enhancing and they revealed the evidence. Do you think she knew what she was seeing?" Mag tapped the license plate on the photo. "And confronted Bryer with the information?"

"The only person who can say for certain is Bryer, and he'd be an idiot to admit to any wrongdoing since he seems to be getting away with it. The man must be made out of four-leaf clovers because he doesn't strike me as having criminal mastermind potential."

Mimicking Mag's enlarging motion in reverse, Clara returned the photo to its normal size and set it aside. "If we're going to bring him to justice, we need a plan, and we need to act fast before he tries to finish what he started with Leanne."

"She's safe enough in the hospital for tonight, and I do my best thinking on a full stomach." With a wink, Mag made for the kitchen, leaving Clara with no other option but to follow.

Realizing she was hungry now herself, Clara raided the refrigerator for leftover chicken and salad ingredients. Meanwhile, Mag grabbed the first thing that came to hand, tossed a loaf of bread on the table, and selected a jar from the pantry.

Halfway through dicing a tomato, Clara looked up, saw the combination of things her sister had spread on slices of pumpernickel, and shuddered.

"That is disgusting," she said, "Don't tell me you're actually going to eat that."

"What's wrong with it? I like peanut butter and liverwurst." She waved the completed sandwich toward her sister, then took a seat at the table. "Now, what are we going to do about Bryer Mack? It's in his best interests to keep his big mouth shut, so the only way I can see of getting a confession out of him is by force."

"Force? So you're advocating what? Casting a truth spell on him? Torture? That's more than a step over the line."

"Of course I don't want to torture the jerk. Not much. Maybe a little. He's killed twice; don't you think we should rough him up a bit?"

"Tempting as that sounds," she said, waggling her finger, "you know that's not our way. Harm none."

Mag crinkled her forehead and heaved a put-upon sigh. "You won't let me torture him, and I'm not allowed to put a truth spell on the man. What other options do we have? I know we're supposed to be laying low while we're in Harmony, but this is an unusual circumstance. Besides, getting him to confess to us won't solve anything. We need to get him to admit what he's done to the authorities."

"No spells."

Mag took a big bite of her sandwich and Clara's appetite evaporated like raindrops on the hood of a hot car.

She shuddered, her salad all but forgotten. "But I agree we have to do something. Try as I might, I can't get rid of the image of that poor girl falling to her death."

"I know, it's—" Mag fell silent.

"It's what? What's wrong? Are you sick?" Alarm sent Clara's stomach fluttering.

"You just gave me an idea."

Clara replayed the conversation in her head to try to figure out how. "Well, tell me already," she ordered.

Mag did, and when she was done, Clara had to admit the plan was a stroke of genius.

***

Purple twilight faded into the silver-tipped night under a pregnant moon by the time all the pieces and players were assembled. Adrenaline sent a delicious tingle through Mag's veins, fed the base of power coiled in her belly, sharpened her senses to a fine point. She'd missed this. The thrill of the hunt, scenting the wind for the telltale sign of prey.

Clara wanted to know why and if and how her sister had chosen to spend so many years in solitary pursuit of that which was a stain on the name of witch. How could she explain the hunt was like food and water? A necessary thing.

Bryer Mack was no Raythe, the fragmented magic of a half-born witch, but he carried the seeds of death with his choices. It was long past time he paid his debt and Mag wanted to be the one to hand him the bill. Compassion for the dead drove Clara, but it was the hard edge of justice Mag craved. And Bryer Mack was about to get his.

Hidden in the moon-cast shadow of the clock face, Mag's eyes glittered at the sound of footsteps on the sidewalk below.

"Get ready." She warned in a low tone. "Stick to the plan, and don't try anything fancy."

"This is going to be fun," Hagatha's voice creaked in the darkness, but she made no promise to reign herself in.

"Bryer! I'm so glad to see you." Trying to sound helpless, Mag called down from the height of the clock tower. "I came up here to look at the town by moonlight, and I must have bumped the lock because the door won't open. Can you help?" The hint of panic elicited a quiet snort from Hagatha.

"I'll be right up." Mag leaned over to watch him disappear through the side door. When it slammed behind him, she whistled the agreed-upon signal to Clara and heard the answering whistle in return. The stage was set, the audience moving into place. Curtain time.

The door handle rattled once, then again, and a third time even harder. "It's stuck. I'll just give it a shove." The next sounds she heard were a thud, and a groan of pain as Bryer slammed his shoulder trying to pop the door open.

If it was mean-spirited for Mag to hold her jamming spell those few extra seconds, she felt no regret at all.

"Can you double check it's not locked from that side?" Bryer called through the door.

"Where's the light switch? I'm working blind in here."

"Left of the door, about midway along the wall. Stand back. I'm going to try again."

Clara gave the all clear, and Mag dropped the spell and let Bryer burst through the door.

"Thanks! I thought I might be stuck here all night." An artfully shaking hand grasped Bryer's as Mag led him to the spot where he needed to be.

"Where's your daughter? I thought she was the one who called and asked me to come help unpack the boxes of commemorative papers. Just lucky Leanne managed to save the day and get them shipped in time."

Another lie in a long list of them.

"No, it was me. Clara was busy tonight, and people say our voices sound similar on the phone. Must be a mother-daughter thing. Shall we go and get started?"

Rarely does the mouse think he's the one toying with the cat, but Bryer never got the memo. When Mag made a move to go around him toward the stairs, he blocked her.

"How many are coming to help?"

"I'm afraid you're the only person I called. Why? Is there a problem? You did say to call on you if we needed a strong back and you've always been so helpful, but I didn't mean to take up too much of your time. I can manage now that you've gotten me out of a pickle." Half of Bryer's face fell in shadow, while the moonlight played off the grim set of his lips.

"No one knows you're here, then?"

Mag let uncertainty show on her face, "No. Are you all right? You seem upset."

"It's this place. Bad memories and a decision I'm not happy about making. I really am sorry to have to do this because you seem like a nice lady." With one long stride, Bryer loomed over Mag. She took one firm step back and banged her cane on the floor. Once and then again. As the second of the two sharp retorts echoed into silence, Hagatha sprang into action.

***

In the distance, Clara heard Mag's signal and, pretending to be answering the call of a real night bird, responded in kind. She flashed a cheery smile at her startled companion. Then, gently using the arm wound through the crook of his elbow, Clara eased Norm McCreery toward the clock tower while he stared up at the night sky.

"You have an interest in astronomy?" She finally asked when he stumbled over a crack in the sidewalk.

"I was just counting my lucky stars for the chance to walk in the moonlight with you, Clara."

A snort rose up to tempt Clara, but she clamped down to keep it from sneaking out.

"What a lovely thing to say. Do you mind if we sit for a minute?" Dropping her hand, she walked through a patch of grass silvered by moonlight and trusted the extra sway in her hips to pull the mayor with her. She moved toward a park bench situated in the one spot where they could sit and hear what would soon happen above them, but not see anything that might betray Hagatha's magic. McCreery might have an inkling about the magical community in his town, but she wasn't going to be the one to give him irrefutable proof.

"I just love listening to the sounds of the night, don't you?"

"Clara, I—" The sound of Mag's cane against weathered wood cracked the night.

"Shh," she touched a finger to his lips. "Just listen."

***

With unpredictable grace, Hagatha Crow circled through the darkness and whipped a scrap of cloth off the silvery slice of ulexite positioned in the path of a moonbeam. Her voice

165

swelled with a whispered harmony of echoes as she breathed an incantation into the air. As the last hissing sound died away, light speared out in both directions from the stone, arced to the next in line, and completed a circle inside the area behind the clock face.

"What's that? What's happening?" Forgetting about Mag for a moment, Bryer whirled to see if he could pinpoint the source of the sound. "I don't—" A hiccuping intake of breath stole the rest of whatever he was going to say when the image of Blossom shivered into being.

Lithe and lean, she flipped up onto the balcony rail and danced along the dangerous edge with the perfect balance of a gymnast. Even knowing this was not the tragic moment of her demise, Mag felt the urge to leap forward and pull the ghostly figure back from danger.

From that distance, she could see Gertrude's estimation of the young woman carried no exaggeration. Fair of face with lively eyes and a gentle smile, Blossom lived up to the sweetness of her name.

Until, at Hagatha's unspoken command, the scene sped up.

"No! Please." A low moan issued from Bryer as he watched Blossom turn wary as she greeted the ghostly image of a younger version of himself stepping out of the shadows.

"Tell me what happened on that night." The order, gently given, carried not even a whisper of magic. Bryer wouldn't need to be forced because his conscience was dying to tell the story. As part of him planned to kill her anyway, Mag let him unload in his own time.

"This was her favorite place, so I knew she would come up here on the night before her wedding, and I waited. All I wanted to do was talk. I swear I never meant to hurt her."

166

"But that's not what happened is it, Bryer?" Mag asked, her voice low.

There was no need for him to answer as they watched the scene play out: Blossom's surprise at seeing Bryer there, the naked yearning on his earnest face, the question that burst from him. *Do you love him?* Her answer. *Yes.*

The pain and the fury welling up in him and the desperate move to pull her close, to kiss lips that hardened against his. Blossom pulling away, waving her hands in anger. *What is wrong with you?*

Beyond reason, Bryer reached for her again and then it happened. Evading him, she'd paid too little attention to her surroundings. She danced away, her movements too fast and too hard to stop the inevitable.

Already knowing how this would end, Mag trained her eyes on the flesh and bone man as he watched the memory play out.

"I killed her. I killed Blossom," Bryer's face crumpled.

Chapter Twenty

Upon hearing Bryer's confession, Mayor McCreery's mouth dropped open in astonishment. He was about to spring into action when Clara shushed him and held him back with a firm grip on his forearm. "Let him finish. She'll make sure he doesn't get away."

Tense shoulders hovering around his ears, the mayor sank back onto the bench to listen. Pale moonlight slanting across his face cast his eyes into shadows deep enough they looked like holes in his face.

"I loved Blossom, truly," Bryer said, his voice cracking with desperation. "It broke my heart when she came back with Dylan. I'd waited for years. Never even looked at another woman. More than anything, I wanted her to be happy. At least, that's what my head said. But my heart felt differently. "

"That night, I had my bag packed for my trip. I didn't want to stick around for the wedding; even the thought made me sick. I was just getting on my bike when I saw her twirling around up in the clock tower, and decided I couldn't leave without at least telling her how I felt about her. She needed to know, and I thought maybe if she remembered the bond we'd shared, she might change her mind, so I blurted out that I loved her." His fists clenched and loosened, then clenched again.

"I'll never forget the look on her face—it wasn't love she felt, but pity. I could see it in her eyes, but I didn't care, and I did something stupid, something desperate; I kissed her."

Watching it all play out in front of her, Mag saw it happen just like he said. Young Bryer, the fire of passion kindling in his eyes, grabbed Blossom and planted one on her. A different kind of passion overcame her as she pushed out of his embrace, her arms waving in the air while she railed at him, and being typical of his gender, Bryer thought that meant he should try again.

The second time, his hands clutched at her arms, and she had to try harder to get away. The momentum sent her backward with too much force.

"It was an accident; I didn't push her, but I killed her just the same."

Bryer's breath hitched and he paused, his eyes glazed over at the painful memory.

"Blossom was still alive by the time I got down to where she landed. I tried to leave, to call an ambulance, but I could tell they were going to be too late. I told her how sorry I was, and her last words to me were *I know*." Hoarse now, he barely got the words out.

"I felt the life go out of her, and I panicked. Just took off and pretended to have left the night before."

Bryer's pain and remorse, though evident, did nothing to quell Mag's need for justice. Had he not gone on to murder again, she might have considered offering him a fraction of the forgiveness Blossom had displayed. Then again, maybe not.

"And what about Marsha Hutchins? She break your heart too? And Leanne Snow? What did she ever do to you?" Mag demanded, drawing out the information she needed—the information she knew was being fed straight to Mayor McCreery.

169

"I never meant to hurt anyone with that fire. In fact, I never meant to hurt anyone at all. I saw the layout Marsha was putting together for the commemorative edition, and I just knew someone was going to see my bike in that photo and connect the dots. When I stopped by the office that night, I thought I could get her to pick a different one. Marsha didn't take the suggestion and began to get suspicious. I saw realization dawn on her face, and I knew I was done for. She wouldn't let go of the photos and tried to run away from me, out the back door.

"She fell. I know you won't believe me, but that's what happened." Rising to swipe through his hair, Bryer's hand trembled.

"When her head hit the corner of the printer and she went still, I knew I had a choice to make. I couldn't stand the idea of having the cops swarming all over me. Couldn't stomach the thought of a trial, of having to rehash everything I'd done."

Useless sniveling weasel, Mag thought and longed to hit him with a series of spells. She pictured him covered in pus-filled boils and felt slightly better.

With no idea he rode the edge of her temper or what Mag's temper made her capable of doing to him, Bryer continued, "Earlier, Leanne had mistaken me for Perry, and when Marsha was lying on the floor, it seemed like fate had dealt me an opportunity. Nobody need know I'd been anywhere near the office that night."

A set of headlights lit the shadows as a car turned down Main Street, and picked out a glitter of tears on his face. The sight of them might have softened Clara's heart, but Mag's remained hard as steel.

"I chose self-preservation like anyone else would. Staging an accident had worked for me once, so I carried her to the bridge and let her fall."

Mag resisted the urge to upchuck her peanut butter and liverwurst, and instead spit vim and vinegar, "She was still alive, wasn't she?"

"I think so," Bryer whispered before finishing his story. "When I found out the paper was still going to print, I tried to destroy the evidence. I had no idea Leanne was inside the building when I started that fire. I never meant to hurt her." His eyes flashed and then turned black as he trained them on Mag's frail body. "Unfortunately, I can't say the same for you."

Bryer made a move to lunge at Mag, but unlike the other women he'd harmed, she saw it coming and was prepared to fight back. Wishing Blossom and Marsha had possessed even a fraction of the power she had at her disposal, Mag whispered a command to the wind. At her bidding, the air thickened, slowing Bryer as he lunged. He saw the smile on her face as she lifted her cane, and rapped him on the head with the polished handle, but could do nothing to stop the blow.

When asked later how it happened, he refused to admit he'd been taken down by an old lady. Nonetheless, Bryer Mack hit the floor with a thud.

When Clara burst into the clock tower on Mayor McCreery's heels moments later, Mag stood over Bryer's prone form with a mixture of pity and disgust dripping off her face.

"What happened?" The Mayor looked from Mag to Bryer in disbelief that a seemingly decrepit old woman could have bested a strapping man so handily.

A tiny white lie tripped off her tongue with ease, "He lunged for me, but got tangled up with my cane."

Clara, who watched McCreery's face with interest while he digested the information, thought she detected mild skepticism and an unwillingness to argue, considering a two-time murderer had been handed to him on a silver platter.

171

"I don't know how you managed to wrangle a confession out of him, but you can rest assured he'll be held to the letter of the law. Chief Cobb is on his way, and I'll need you both to make an official statement. You've done this town a great service, and I want you to know that I won't forget it."

With a conspiratorial wink, he dismissed the Balefire sisters, instructing them to wait in the quad while he stood watch over Bryer. Mag almost offered him her cane just in case.

For once, Hagatha had done as she promised and remained hidden in the shadows until Mag and Clara returned to solid ground.

"That was spectacular," she cackled, rubbing her hands together. "I haven't had this much fun in years, and you really came through, Hagatha. Great show," Mag showered praise on Hagatha since, without the ulexite caper, she and Clara would have had no way to expose Bryer's indiscretions.

Clara wholeheartedly agreed. "I know we foiled your plans for the festival, and I hope you'll agree it was for a good cause."

Hagatha nodded, then grinned like a child. "This is certainly going to get Penelope's knickers in a twist. It's us against them now, you know. Poetic justice, I say. Thought they were going to recruit the famous Balefire witches to keep tabs on old Haggie. Thought me a loose cannon, hell-bent on exposing magic to the town of Harmony. Joke's on them!"

"You mean that's not your goal?"

"Heaven's no! All I want is for the witches in my coven to act like, well, *witches*. This nonsense about not doing magic in public is ludicrous. Where do they think we've been practicing for the last few thousand years? Utter hogwash. I don't need babysitters. You can either help me or hinder me, but I'm going to do what I want, when I want. I've earned that right."

Without waiting for a response, Hagatha blinked out of sight, leaving Mag and Clara alone and staring at one another.

***

A tinkling of bells preceded Leanne Snow into Balms and Bygones, and when Mag and Clara looked up from the stack of profit and loss reports they were studying, both sisters had to do a double take. Barely recognizable, Leanne had finally begun the transformation of Clara's wishes. Where once a caterpillar timidly meandered from one bit of camouflage to the next, a butterfly now proudly flitted, exposing her beautiful wings for all the world to see.

Gone was the troweled-on makeup and the guarded expression of a woman who doubts her worth; for the first time, Leanne looked comfortable in her own skin, and her easy smile even put a lump in Mag's throat.

"Hello, you two." Her voice was still slightly scratchy, but had markedly improved in the few days since Bryer's arrest and her release from the hospital. "Dylan's been keeping me under lock and key since I got home, but he fell asleep while putting the baby down for a nap so I took advantage of the situation. I wanted to come and thank you in person."

Clara crossed the room in three strides, and treated Leanne to a warm hug. "No thanks necessary. We're just happy you're all right. You look amazing, by the way."

Mag surprised Leanne, Clara, and even herself a little bit when she stepped forward and mimicked Clara's gesture, wrapping her arms somewhat awkwardly around Leanne.

"We heard Marsha's cousin decided to take on management of the newspaper office. The Harmony Holler will live to see another day."

Leanne's mouth turned up into a gleeful smile. "You know what? I quit. And I couldn't be more thrilled to start a new chapter in my life. Dylan just got a big promotion at work, and he said he'd rather I not return to that office after everything that's happened."

"Does that mean Perry's planning to rebuild?" The idea of supplying him with vintage office furniture lifted Mag's spirits.

"He is, and Marsha's cousin will be taking over Harmony Holler. I think it's a fitting tribute to her memory." Leanne's let a crooked grin hold back sentiment long enough to keep from tearing up again.

"Besides," she grinned again, "If I get bored, I could always join your Moonstone Circle, you know, give back to the community."

"It's not as much fun as it looks," Mag offered her personal point of view.

"How can you say that? This year's celebration was positively magical."

The End

174

Made in the USA
Middletown, DE
07 July 2018